Str

The path was dusty and rutted. It would lead them through the donkey field, past the new housing estate and the infant school, and on up the hill to their home.

'Come on, Steven.' Elaine set off again as soon as her brother had pulled himself over the tip of the slope. For a moment he lay on the grass at the side of the path, listening to the thud of her feet. Far away he could hear the drone of the city, like a hushed roar. The sound never stopped, day and night. It was the sound of foundries, hammering like a heart. It was the sound of cars and lorries and buses, always on the move, like blood pumping through veins. It was the sound of half a million people breathing.

Streets Ahead

Edited by Valerie Bierman

MAMMOTH

To my family –
especially Michael, Paul and Louise

First published 1989
by Methuen Children's Books
Published 1990 by Mammoth
an imprint of Mandarin Paperbacks
Michelin House, 81 Fulham Road, London SW3 6RB
Reprinted 1992

Mandarin is an imprint of the Octopus Publishing Group,
a division of Reed International Books Limited

'Owls are Night Birds' by Berlie Doherty has been
broadcast on BBC Radio 4 Morning Story and an
abbreviated version has been published by Nelson.

'The Mystery of the Beehive' by Bernard MacLaverty
from *Storyline Scotland 4*. Wide Range Series
(published by Oliver & Boyd 1985), appears with kind
permission of the Longman Group UK Limited.

ISBN 0 7497 0297 4

A CIP catalogue record for this title
is available from the British Library

Printed in Great Britain
by Cox & Wyman Ltd, Reading, Berkshire

Contents

Introduction

CITY. What does it make you think of? If you don't live in one, you probably think it's a mixture of London and Dallas, all bright lights, trendy shops and places to visit. If you live in a city, you know that in reality life is more likely to be bus queues, crowded supermarkets, lifts that don't work and nowhere to play.

As so many of us live in cities nowadays, I wanted to see how different writers would interpret the lives of children living in a city. I wanted a short story – brief enough to perhaps read aloud, talk about and think about. It had to be three thousand words long, unlike a novel which can be up to sixty thousand words long. You might think it's easier to write less – but you try it – it isn't! So I approached ten writers – all well known for their novels, several for their adult novels, too, and asked them to write a story on any theme that interested them – provided it had a city as a background. The results were exciting – and sometimes surprising.

I knew that Michael Hardcastle wouldn't resist the temptation to contribute a sports story – and he didn't. And I suspected that Londoner born and bred Terrance Dicks would use that city as a background – and he did! Two stories are set, quite coincidentally in Edinburgh where I live, but it's perhaps not so surprising when authors Joan Lingard and Anne Fine live there too. As for the other stories, several have backgrounds close to the author's home or childhood home like Bernard MacLaverty's Belfast or Ann Pilling's Lancashire. Rhodri Jones has lived in both Glasgow and London, but uses his experience as a London comprehensive school teacher in his story.

They are a fascinating mixture – some will make you laugh, like Gene Kemp's contribution, which also shows it's not always easy to get yourself out of a tricky situation! If you want an eerie read, then Alison Prince's Bonfire Night tale will have you thinking. Many of the authors use the theme of the dangers of the city, dangers which you probably see in a completely different way from your parents. Is life really as bad as the papers say? There are certainly muggings and robberies but at least we don't have the blitz to worry about any more! Perhaps one of the most scary things today is watching helplessly as the countryside is gobbled up by the city – a very frightening thing. Berlie Doherty's story shows the effect this has on both children, adults and wild life. It's set in a place very similar to the one in which I grew up – a community surrounded by fields between two large industrial towns. I too visited a shop which was the front room of a house to choose sweets, ice-cream or biscuits and sometimes a library book carefully selected from a battered case behind a curtain. Now there's a motorway through the fields, my school on the hill is in the middle of a housing estate and no one rides on the farmer's hay cart any more, or watches him deliver milk to the jug on your doorstep.

But cities can be exciting places – if you know where to look. There are all kinds of museums, galleries and libraries, parks and gardens and if you're lucky, a city farm. Use these stories to discover things too. Read other books by the authors – think about the children in the stories. There's plenty to talk about. Begin at the beginning, middle or the end – it doesn't matter. It's a book for dipping into and most of all, for enjoying.

Valerie Bierman
Edinburgh July 1988

A Few Miaows about

Gene Kemp

by Scroggins, the Wonder Cat

I am a very handsome cat in black and white with fine whiskers and a velvety coat. Gene Kemp is one of my slaves. She could be worse, though I do wish she appreciated the presents I give her, such as dead mice and birds. When she's not busy opening and shutting doors for me I allow her to write these peculiar things called books.

Of course all these books should be about ME. But she says she must put children in them. However, she wrote some stories about a Tamworth Pig. *Her best known one is a school book called* The Turbulent Term of Tyke Tiler – *there's a dog in that, huh! Then* Gowie Corby Plays Chicken *has a pet rat in it!* Charlie Lewis Plays for Time *has lots about music (I sing beautifully, myself). There are two ghostly ones:* The Clock Tower Ghost *and* Jason Bodger and the Priory Ghost. No Place Like *is about a Sixth Form college. I don't recommend* Crocodile Dog – *a disgusting animal.*

But Juniper *has a real hero of a cat in it. And* Dog Days *and* Cat Naps – *smashing.* The Well *has a kitten in it, I'm glad to say. But, children, what I want to know is this: why doesn't she write about me?*

SCROGGINS – THE WONDER CAT

A Bad Day in El Dorado

Once we'd got rid of Sharon it was OK, Marie said. We could do what we liked then. Sharon's our eldest sister – fifteen and bossy with it – Mum said we had to stay together all the time we were in the park because you never knew these days with muggers, murderers and worse on the lurk everywhere ready to pounce on the defenceless, even on little Ems – only twelve months old – and always asleep except when crawling all over the place, eating everything, anything.

Sharon was mad at this. She didn't want us any more than we wanted *her*.

'Why should I land that horrible bunch every holiday?' she shouted. 'It's not fair.'

'The sooner you find that life isn't fair the better you'll get on with it,' said Mum. 'And with me,' she added.

'What about my course work? I've got all the last bits to sort out. It's to be handed in any day *now*. You don't seem to realise.'

'You can get on with it when you come back in. You won't be all day at the park. Just make sure you keep an eye on them *there*.'

'I used to go to the park on my own. Why can't they?'

'Because things were different then. It's a wicked time today. I daren't let my kids out of sight now. Especially Ems.'

My mum's tough with us but Ems is the apple of her eye. Ems can do no wrong, though as far as I can see she doesn't do anything right. If ever there was a juvenile delinquent – I think they call them that – at twelve months, it's Ems. But enough of her.

Mum went. We watched telly for a bit, then Sharon dressed Ems, shrieking and kicking all the way as she hates clothes. Then we set off, Sharon, Marie, me and Ems and Slug. Slug isn't *us*, of course. We wouldn't own him in our family, but he's always around because he's an only, living next door.

'Have we got to have him?' groaned Sharon. Slug is called Slug for a simple reason. He looks like one. Pale, oozy and squelchy. His personality does not make up for his looks. That's pale, oozy and squelchy, as well.

'If we don't have him, no one else will,' I said.

'So? Can't he just be put down?' Sharon asked, hard as nails from her spiky hair to her booted feet.

Slug wobbled hopefully at us.

'He's coming,' said my other sister, Marie, you remember. And Sharon shrugged and left it.

'OK. OK. As long as he doesn't come near me.'

So Slug trailed along behind, and I dropped back too, because however yuck he is, and he is, very, at least he's another boy in the female-filled world I live in. You've got an idea what Sharon's like. But *Marie* – well, worse is not the word for Marie. I tell you, at times she terrifies me.

'The pretty one,' people say. That's not difficult, what with Ems looking like a Martian and Sharon a gangster. But Marie's all hair and dreaming eyes. She makes up alternative worlds for us; her adventures, she calls them. 'I must have adventures. I can't live without adventures,' she cries, completely barmy.

Oh, she's nice to me. Not like Sharon. When I was little at school, she'd stick up for me, and she'd fight to her last little toe for any of her family or a friend. But what scares me about her is this:

What will she do next?

What will she get *me* to do next?

Climb our tower block at the end of the street? Go into that empty church that is supposed to be haunted at midnight? Set up on Razor Gillet when he's beating up that kid brother of his, *again*?

You get the message. 'Go on, Gary, you know you can do it. GO ON GARY!' And afterwards?

My mother shouting: 'And what on earth made you do a daft, crazy thing like that for?'

And when I say, 'Marie told me . . . ' she doesn't believe me. No one does.

But enough of that. There we were on a warm morning going to the park: Sharon in front, trying to look as if she wasn't with us; Ems asleep in the buggy pushed by Marie (Ems sleeps like an angel all the time it's on the move, the trouble begins if you stop); and Slug oozing along, with me just ahead of him.

Somewhere along the way Marie handed over buggy-pushing to me and vanished – to pop up a couple of streets later, whistling happily. She gave me a bit of gum and took over the buggy.

And at the park, who should be waiting there, kicking the bottom steps of the helter-skelter but Mike Andrews, who Sharon's been fancying ever since she got rid of the last one whose name I forget. He turned to watch us as we made our way across the grass and Marie winked one of her great big saucers at me so I knew she'd wangled something again.

'He got here fast,' she muttered out of the side of her mouth, in case Sharon heard, but she was too busy almost not running to where the beloved stood kicking and grunting at the foot of the blue and red helter-skelter.

'Love's Young Dream,' burbled Slug.

'Shut up,' Marie and I both said.

'There I told you,' she went on.

'How did you do it?'

'Phoned him, of course. He couldn't get here quick enough.'

'Like I said. Love's . . .' began Slug.

'Shut up,' we shouted.

Ems stirred. Marie rattled the buggy a bit.

'We can do what *we* want. Without her . . .' Marie murmured dreamily. 'Come on.'

'Where are we going?' I asked, already scared. 'Let's stay here.'

'Oh, no. Boring, boring.'

'*Where* are we going?'

'El Dorado.'

'Oh, no. We can't.'

'We can.'

'Mum said we weren't to, *ever*.'

'She won't know,' said my sister, Marie.

She shouted to Sharon.

'We're off, then.'

Sharon didn't bother to answer.

'Marie. Slug and I don't wanna go. I like the swings. And the Indian hut. And the pool's full. It's hot. We can go in the pool.'

'El Dorado's much better. Besides, I've bought goodies to eat when we get there.'

'No.'

'It'll be OK, I tell you. It's always OK with me, isn't it?'

'No. It isn't always OK with you. Is it, Slug?'

He slimed up near to us, happy at being spoken to. But Marie smiled into his eyes, which no one ever does to Slug, so he turned dirty orange-mauve and I knew I'd get no support from him. Then she handed him a chocolate drop, which Ems spotted and screamed violently because someone else was getting her chocky drops. So Marie popped one in her wide open gate – sorry, mouth, Mum says not to use 'gate' – and began to whirl the buggy across the park at enormous speed, especially considering the wheels which always jam when I do that causing it to travel sideways or backwards. Once more Ems fell asleep.

'I wanted to go on something,' I shouted, keeping up.

'Tough.'

'We could paddle in the pool.'

'This'll be better. It'll be real.'

'Pete's sake. The pool's real enough. And it's hot, now.'

'You know what Ems is like. She'll want to go in too and scream the place down. Then she'll pee in the water and everyone'll be mad at us. Then Sharon will think she'd better take some notice of us. We don't want all that, do we?'

'No,' I panted doubtfully. 'But do we have to go to El Dorado?'

Arguing was a waste of time. We pounded past the adventure playground, the concrete tunnels, the roundabout, the benches under the trees, the little houses saying Ladies and Gentlemen, past the cypress trees and out of the back gate, down the secret alleyway, through the back garden of the Four Horseshoes and then the dustbinny alleyway at the back of Razor Gillet's place.

'Quiet here.'

And then suddenly we were jumped, shock, horror, even if we were expecting it. Down from the walls dropped one in front, two behind, us in the middle, oh no, it's the end, I thought. Slug squeaked.

But it wasn't Razor. He wouldn't waste time on us anyway, I hope. It was only his kid brother trying to play 'menace' with his mates. No match for Marie.

'S-C-R-A-M. Beat it,' she bellowed, charging them with the buggy as a battering ram. As they fled she rounded on the one behind Slug but he legged it as fast as he could.

'RUBBISH,' shouted Marie, jumping up and down, slapping her hands. Ems hadn't even woken up.

Then the Pelican crossing, shops on the right, traffic snarling and a gateway in the wall in a corner sheltered by an ancient tree. The gate looked as if it was padlocked but with a twist Marie opened it just as she had the first time. We'd gone again and then once more but that last time someone saw us and told Mum.

Forbidden.

We'd obeyed her. Till now.

'We're there,' Marie sighed. 'El Dorado.'

She twiddled the padlock and we were through. The traffic's noise slid away from us. Sun poured through the leaves into the green valley below. A pavilion/summerhouse thing – oh, I don't know what it's called – glinted gold in the sunlight welcoming us, almost smiling at us as it did when we saw it that first day and Marie called out, 'It's El Dorado!'

'What?'

'El Dorado. A place of gold. We've found our "place of gold".'

'Grub first. Then we'll play.'

We found a level spot on the green grass. Ems woke up and we all tucked in. Marie let Slug give Ems her bottle. He turns mauve-orange with happiness if Marie allows him to hold her. It's a nasty sight but it saves me doing it. Then Marie fastened Ems in the buggy and we played, for by then it didn't matter any more that we weren't supposed to be there, that it was forbidden.

We climbed the grey and white stones and rocks, and swung from the rope we'd hung on one of the huge trees growing at the side of the pool. Then we did Marie's version of St George killing the Dragon and rescuing the Princess. Hers is much the same except the Princess (Marie) kills the Dragon (Slug) and rescues me (the Knight). The pavilion place makes a smashing cave for the dragon to come roaring out of, and Slug's not bad at that. He died quite well, too. The pavilion floor's really quite safe, Marie says, though some of the boards are missing. A fantastic place full of treasures – that's where we got the rope for swinging on, and there's an old sofa and a bike and a box full of things like swords – that's how Marie came to think of the Dragon game. The whole valley is full of things, but we're careful. We never play with the old fridge that's been left down here, for instance, 'cos Mum's warned us over and over not to get in fridges and close the doors.

But at last we were worn out, finished, splat. And then I noticed something or rather I noticed a nothing.

'Ems is quiet. Must be asleep,' I said.

She'd been screaming blue murder at first because she was in the buggy while we were playing and Slug had worried about her, but Marie popped in a few melty choc drops and she settled a bit.

'I'll let her out of the buggy,' Marie said, turning round.

The buggy was empty.

I tell you this was one of the all-time bad moments of my life. Marie's face turned chalk-white. Slug made a strange whiffling noise through his nose.

'The pool,' he gulped.

We rushed to the pool. Nothing there. Back to the buggy where the reins lay empty.

'I didn't fasten her in properly,' Marie said, and a tear began to slide down her cheek.

'She's gotta be somewhere. I know it,' I said.

'Ems! Ems! Ems! Ems! Ems!'

El Dorado echoed.

Like mad things we ran through the grass, up and down the hills, round the trees, behind the rocks, crying, shouting, in a dream, no, a nightmare. Ems lost for ever. Mum. Don't think about Mum.

'Ems! Ems! Ems!'

Squawks sounded from behind the old pavilion.

Ems only has three noises and a squawk's one of them.

Like Olympic athletes, we sped towards the noise. Ems, gurgling and squawking, was attacking a packet of biscuits, just beginning to tear a bit of paper off the packet. Ems was happy. Beside her, cushioned by a mossy bank, her bag of groceries spilt on the ground, lay fat old Mrs Birkenshaw who lives next door, on the other side of Slug.

I stared at Mrs Birkenshaw.

'She's dead,' I said.

Marie seized Ems, who shrieked and struggled, then plonked her down with a biscuit. Ems immediately got stuck into it.

'She's dead,' I said again.

'Stop saying that!' cried Marie.

'She looks dead,' Slug said.

'How would you know? She can't be dead.'

Marie bent over her and shook her shoulder – she must be brave, I couldn't have touched the old lady.

'Mrs Birkenshaw, wake up. Come on. Wake up. You don't want to go to sleep here.'

Mrs Birkenshaw did not wake up.

'Ems took your biscuits, but she didn't mean to, did you, Ems?' Marie went on, her voice rising higher, and trembling a bit.

Slug peered closely at Mrs Birkenshaw's face.

'She's an awful colour.'

'Even worse than yours,' agreed Marie. 'Mrs Birkenshaw!'

'Is she moving a bit?'

'No.'

'Some water from the pond?'

'What for?'

'To wake her up.'

'I think she's dead.'

'No, she's not. She's breathing a bit. Listen.'

We listened and looked. Mrs Birkenshaw was indeed breathing a bit, not good breathing but better than nothing at all, a kind of flutter.

'Can we move her?'

We looked at her. A big woman Mrs Birkenshaw, even when on the move. Very big, flat out on a mossy bank in El Dorado with her grocery bag.

'I don't think so.'

'We must fetch somebody,' said Slug.

'We can't.'

'Why not, Marie?'

'And get in a row for being here? We need to move her to the gate and then someone will help. Come on. Everybody find a bit and pull her up.'

'No. We can't,' I said.

'No. We can't,' said Slug.

'I know we can't,' said Marie. We stood and eyed one another. Then we eyed Mrs Birkenshaw.

'Just let's go,' I suggested. 'Somebody's bound to come along and find her.'

Slug looked at me like other people look at him. So I tried again.

'Marie, ring 999 and tell them where she is and we'll push off.'

Well, it didn't seem to be a bad idea.

Slug looked at me – even worse. Marie ignored me.

'It's all right,' she said at last. 'I've thought about telling Mum. It will just have to be done and I'll say it was my fault. I'm going now to ring 999 and I want you to stay here and look after Mrs Birkenshaw and Ems.'

'Sharon will get into trouble as well.' I tried to cheer her.

She looked at me in a way that told me I was not flavour of the month.

'David,' she said to Slug (that's his real name). 'I know I can trust you. Watch the old lady. You,' she meant me, 'try not to lose Ems.'

'I didn't lose her last time,' I said, but no one was listening, so I turned to Ems who was fine. She'd never been let loose with a whole packet of custard creams before. Slug sat with his hand on the old lady's. After a bit he went to the pool, dipped his hanky in it and bathed her forehead.

'That won't do much good. Not your rotten filthy noserag.'

He didn't answer.

Marie came back with a police person, Katy Simmons, who lives two doors down from Mrs Birkenshaw.

'Hello David. Hello Gary. Hello Ems. Oh, poor old lady.'

She bent over Mrs Birkenshaw.

'You found her here just like this?'

'Yes. Ems found her biscuits. Sorry. You needn't have let her have *all* of them, Gary.'

'What was she doing here, Katy?'

'Well, long ago, there used to be a path here. It was a short cut. Perhaps she tried to walk home, felt funny and fell. She hasn't been mugged.'

'Only Ems, with the biscuits.'

'Shut up.'

I could say nothing right.

'The ambulance is coming,' said Katy.

'They can't drive down here.'

'No, they'll bring a stretcher. And Marie, what were all of *you* doing down here? Or shouldn't I ask?' Katy had turned into PC Simmons.

Silence.

'There's a NO ENTRY sign and DANGER on the gate,' went on PC Simmons.

'It's turned round so you can't see it,' muttered Marie.

'Oh, I wonder who did that?'

'I did,' said Marie.

'And fiddled the padlock.'

'Yes.'

Two men with a stretcher came into view. With two others they lifted the fat old lady on to it and covered her with blankets.

'Will she be all right?' sniffed Slug.

'Hope so.'

'She's a fair old weight,' said one of them as they went up the hill.

PC Simmons turned to us, her face very serious.

'I'll tell you what I'll do. I'll put in a word for you and say how sensible you've been and if the old lady lives it'll be thanks to you . . . .'

'Oh, thank you . . . .'

'In return, you promise never to come here again.'

Marie looked all around El Dorado, her eyes more than ever like saucers.

'Not ever?'

'Not ever. Actually the Council has it scheduled for something or other – in the meantime it's forbidden. The whole place could be a death trap. The pavilion's rotten, there's rubbish everywhere, the pool's very deep and they say someone's been dumping chemicals here as well as old bikes, fridges etc. It's a dreadful place, so keep away. Play in the park.'

But the saucers had brimmed over with tears flowing everywhere.

'But it's so beautiful. I love it,' wept Marie.

'Why? This old dump. It's awful. Look, Marie, if you love something pretty come and look at my patio some time. I've got lots of flowers and . . .'

But Marie just cried and cried.

'I think you're just scared of what your mum will say,' said PC Simmons, turning into Katy once more. 'Don't be. Just own up and say you're sorry.'

'No, Katy,' said Slug. 'She's not crying about that. Are you, Marie?'

'Then what are you crying for?'

'The end of magic, of course,' Slug said and Marie nodded as she picked up Ems and fastened her very securely into the buggy.

Ann Pilling

I was brought up in a Lancashire town very like Darnley-in-Makerfield. I had a sister and a brother and one of the things we liked best was to escape from the soot and the smoke to a cottage in Wales where we used to spend our holidays. It was a very old house with a mysterious 'sealed room'. I often wondered what lay behind the wall and I have written all about this in On the Lion's Side. That book also describes my mother. She was a hopeless cook and did the washing about three times a year, but she loved poetry and music. These loves she passed on to me.

At school my best subjects were music and English. I always wanted to be a writer but for years I thought I was going to be a poet. It was when my two sons (Ben and Thomas) started bringing bad books home from school that I decided to try and write a good children's book. That's how my career started. (Ben is Henry, of Henry's Leg, and Thomas is like Terence Bott, in The Big Biscuit). For a time, at school, I was very fat. They used to sing 'Roll out the Barrel' as I came round the corner. I have written about all this in The Big Pink.

Under the name Ann Cheetham I've written four ghost stories. I've always liked the spooky and the gory. When I was eleven I went on a school trip to Belgium and made a secret return visit to an art gallery, to have another look at a painting of someone being skinned alive. I think the chilliest stories are those based on truth and all my ghost books have real facts behind them.

Goosey Goosey Gander *came from an old newspaper story I saw in the* Oxford Times. *The fire happened in the centre of Oxford, in the street where I live but I have transferred it to Darnley.*

Apart from books I like music – listening to it and singing, when nobody else is around – gardening, and walking. I have two sons and two cats. We also have some tropical fish. These live in the front attic where Loll sleeps in the story. They are pretty to look at but you can't take them for walks, can you?

Goosey Goosey Gander

The Bostocks were moving from the pretty Lancashire village of Brampton to a house slap-bang in the middle of the town, and Lawrence and Julia didn't like it one bit.

Julia was ten, and had lots of friends at her primary school. Why go and buy a house miles away in horrible, dirty Darnley-in-Makerfield? You couldn't hear the birds sing there because of all the factory noises, and you had to keep your eyes peeled wherever you went, for fear of walking under a bus. 'It's not *fair*,' she pouted, watching her mother wrap up china in newspaper and pack it in cardboard boxes. 'I hate the new house.'

'I hate it too,' said Lawrence. He was five and he always copied what Julia said. Secretly though, he felt rather excited about moving. It meant he would go to school at last, and he'd been promised his own bedroom too. In the cottage he had to share with Julia. Besides, Great Aunt Annie was already living at the new house and Great Aunt Annie had a sweet tin.

'You can't hate what you've never seen,' Mrs Bostock said wearily. 'Dad's offered to take you to see Baillie Square half a dozen times now it's all been re-decorated, but you just won't go.'

'Well, I still don't think it's fair,' moaned Julia. 'I like the country. Darnley's dirty, and it smells.'

Her mother abandoned her china-wrapping and sat down on the floor. 'Listen,' she said. 'First of all, Darnley doesn't smell, and 19 Baillie Square is a beautiful house. It's all been cleaned up and the factories aren't allowed to have smoking chimneys any more.'

'But I won't have any *friends*. People don't live in places like Baillie Square, right in the middle of towns.'

'That's not true either. There are the Wilkinsons two doors away, and the Shaws just opposite, and the three Vicarage children on the corner . . .'

'Yuk! That's another thing, Aunt Annie'll make us go to church. She's church mad.'

'Remember what the doctor told Dad,' Mrs Bostock reminded her. She'd gone beyond the red-faced arguey stage now and looked all set to burst into tears. 'He ought to give up the long drive into work. It's miles from here to his office, love, and when there's a hold-up on the motorway . . .'

'But why couldn't we just buy somewhere nearer, in another village? Why Darnley? Ugh!' and Julia did cry now.

'Well, it's only an experiment. We're not buying the house from Aunt Annie yet. We're just renting part of it, and if it doesn't work out we can come back here, to Sweet Briars. Dad's only letting the Jacksons use it for a year.'

A year. It felt like for ever to Julia. 'Some experiment!' she said rudely, glaring at all the packing cases. 'I'm going to see Charlotte. It'll probably be my last chance,' and she stormed off.

Lawrence cuddled up to his mother. He didn't like it when Julia shouted. 'Is there a fire station at Aunt Annie's?' he said timidly.

Mrs Bostock hesitated. Just before Christmas he'd

managed to find some matches and started a blaze in the garage. Two fire engines had come over from Heading-ford and he'd been fascinated by them. He'd not under-stood that he could have burned Sweet Briars to the ground, only that two gleaming red trucks and eight men with shiny yellow hats had come tearing up their lane. And all because of him. Since then all matches had been kept hidden. But Lawrence was still fascinated by fire. Only last week they'd caught him fiddling with a cigarette lighter.

'There'll be one in Manchester,' she said cautiously. 'That's a very big city. We could go there on the bus. There are lots of shops in Manchester, and cinemas, and a skating rink, and there's a famous orchestra called the Hallé.'

But his glassy eyes told her that he'd not heard one word about Manchester. All he cared about was living near the fire station.

'I can smell something burning,' Dad said. 'Have you left the milk pan on, Auntie?' It was eleven o'clock and Mr and Mrs Bostock were having a late night drink down in the basement flat. Julia was there too. Her official bedtime was eight-thirty, but she came down most evenings complaining that she couldn't sleep. She'd started off in the big back attic, next to Lawrence, but that had only lasted a week. Her bedroom was on the floor below now, next to Mum and Dad. She said she felt 'safer' there.

'Safe from what?' Dad had said rather grumpily, watching Mum trying to manoeuvre a mattress down the narrow attic stairs. He wasn't allowed to lift heavy things, since his illness.

Julia wouldn't tell, except that she thought Aunt Annie's had a 'creepy feeling'.

'Stuff and nonsense. It's a lovely old house.'

Great Aunt Annie was eighty-one. She was still very fit but she did get muddled about things. 'It'll be them students,' she said, as Dad went to investigate the smell. 'They're up at all hours, cooking.' The Bostocks exchanged glances. Four students from the Polytechnic had rented rooms at 19 Baillie Square last year but they'd left months ago.

'I'll just go up and check in our kitchen then, Auntie,' Dad said. 'There's certainly nothing on in yours.' And he climbed the stairs to the ground floor. Mum and Julia followed and they all stood together in the long narrow hall with its pattern of black and white tiles, tiles that had been washed morning and evening years ago, by a little servant girl, according to Aunt Annie. She'd been born in the house, and her father before her.

The smell was stronger here. Julia ran into the front room where they'd had a fire burning in the grate. But nothing remained of it except a heap of reddish ash and anyhow, the big fire-guard was firmly in position.

'It's upstairs,' Mum said, turning very pale all of a sudden. 'It's . . . *Lawrence!*' And she began to mount the staircase, two steps at a time.

Julia shoved past and was in the attic before her mother had reached the second-floor landing. Dad, who wasn't supposed to rush anywhere, made his way up more slowly.

'Well there's nothing burning,' Julia said, coming out of the tiny back bedroom. 'It's all OK in here, and Loll's fast asleep.'

Nothing could be seen of Lawrence except a little mound of bedding. The room smelt of fresh paint and wallpaper but the scorching, burning smell was much stronger now.

'There must be a big fire in town,' Dad said, puffing slightly as he appeared at the top of the stairs. 'I didn't hear any sirens though.'

'Well, Loll must have because he's *not* in this bed.' Julia had deliberately sat down right in the middle of the hump, just to annoy him, and discovered it was empty.

Mrs Bostock tore back the covers. All she found was a collection of stuffed toys, half a biscuit and an old comic. He wasn't in the attic and he wasn't in the rooms down below. Loll had vanished into thin air.

Back in the hall Dad pulled open the heavy front door and looked out. A small five-year-old surely couldn't have climbed up, unbolted it and slipped through yet he was starting to panic. Loll was drawn to fires like ducks were to water.

As he stood staring up and down the street Great Aunt Annie suddenly rapped on her basement window. Dad looked down the grating in the pavement and saw her smiling, and pointing at something. She'd got Loll in her arms, wrapped up in a blanket, and he was waving a picture book.

'*Lawrence!*' Dad went back inside and took the phone off Mum. She was nearly in tears now, and in the middle of dialling 999. 'It's OK,' he said. 'He was with Aunt Annie. Don't know how on earth he slipped past us.'

'Perhaps he was in that little loo on the second floor landing,' she sniffed. 'He likes that game. I never thought of . . .'

'No he wasn't,' Julia interrupted. 'I looked in there.'

* * *

'Now come on, Loll, this is naughty. You're keeping Aunt Annie out of bed.' Down in the basement sitting-room Dad took him into his arms, restored the tatty nursery rhyme book to its shelf and went to the door. 'I'm sorry, Auntie. This won't happen again.'

'It's all right, chuck, I don't mind. I wasn't in bed any road.'

But Lawrence had started to howl. 'I want to see the lady again, I want to show you that *lady*.'

'Tomorrow. You can come down for a story tomorrow. Listen, we should all be in bed by now, it's nearly midnight.'

'But what about that smell?' Julia started, the minute Aunt Annie's door was closed. Mum, following her up the basement stairs, gave her a sharp dig in the back.

'It was obviously outside,' she whispered. 'It's gone now anyhow. Listen, let's just keep quiet about it. 'I think Loll's getting over that fire thing so the less said at this stage the better.'

Dad was making his way upstairs to put Lawrence back in bed and Julia was following, with her mother. But at the part where the stairs widened out, on the first landing, she suddenly stopped dead.

'Come on, Julia, for heaven's sake. I'm tired. What are you doing?'

'I don't like going past here at night, Mum. This is the creepy part.'

'Darling, it's not a bit "creepy". You love Aunt Annie's old rocking horse don't you? And it's just the place for it on this landing, much better than where it used to be, in that poky back room.' But she'd noticed that Julia never sat on the old black horse now, or threaded ribbons through its mane like she used to.

'I get a funny cold feeling when I go past this bit,' she

said in an embarrassed rush, grabbing at her mother's hand. 'You can say I'm silly, Mum, but I *do*. And I wish we could go back to Sweet Briars like you promised. I don't want to stay here for a whole year, I just *don't*!' And she ran into her bedroom and slammed the door.

Gradually, though, Julia stopped complaining about living at Aunt Annie's. Nearly all the children in the square went to her school and they fell over themselves to be friendly when they knew she was the great-niece of old Annie Birdsall. She'd been on telly last year, on *Look North*. It was her 80th birthday and they'd had her talking about her house in Baillie Square. Her grandfather had bought it when it was brand-new and the Birdsall family had lived in it ever since.

Lawrence loved school. It was nearly all play for the infants and at twelve o'clock Mum took him home for dinner and a little sleep. On his very first Friday he got a book out of the story box called *Our Friend the Fireman*.

Mum frowned when she saw it. She really thought Loll was getting over his fascination with fires but that night she realised she was wrong. There was a sudden terrific smell of burning in the house as she stood in the kitchen, drying the bedtime mugs before going upstairs. All the windows were closed and there'd definitely been no sirens in the street. This time she ran down to Aunt Annie's flat first. The old lady was nodding in her chair, making gentle snoring noises. No fumes down here though, no smoke, no smell, *no Loll*. Mrs Bostock tore up through the house, flinging all the doors open as she went. Her husband was already asleep in the large front bedroom. Julia was asleep, too. There was nothing burning in the back attic though she kicked aside all the empty boxes they'd stored in there, just to make sure, and Lawrence's room was in perfect order for once. She'd given it a good clean-up while he'd been playing in the square that afternoon, with Julia and her new friends.

Even so, she tugged the wobbly old wardrobe away from the wall and looked behind it, pulled out drawers, and ripped back a bit of the carpet in case the floorboards were smouldering, the smell in the room was so overpowering. *Nothing.* But when she turned Lawrence's covers back, to check that he was safe under his usual mound, she found the bed empty. It was just like the first time.

Instinct told her that he'd somehow slipped past and gone down to see Aunt Annie again. The big attraction was her sweet tin and all her old-fashioned picture books. Since the move Mr and Mrs Bostock hadn't had much time for reading to Lawrence, but Great Aunt Annie had all the time in the world. She loved children. Julia got a bit irritated when she repeated all the old Baillie Square stories, and she didn't much like being told to 'say your prayers' every night. Loll didn't mind though. He said little prayers with Auntie Annie, after his story and his sweet.

When Mrs Bostock got down to the basement again she was out of breath. There were fifty-six stairs between Loll's door and Aunt Annie's and she'd run down every one of them. There he was, sitting on his aunt's knee, with the little ginger cat on *his* knee, and they were all looking at nursery rhymes.

'Goosey goosey gander,
Whither shall I wander?
Upstairs and downstairs
And in my lady's chamber . . .'

'That lady, Auntie, *that* lady,' he was jabbering excitedly. 'That one in the funny hat . . .'

When she saw Mrs Bostock Great Aunt Annie looked slightly guilty. 'I'm sorry, chuck,' she said, 'but he just came down, all on his own, and I thought one little story wouldn't hurt, to settle him like.'

'It was a lady brought me,' Lawrence said sleepily, yawning and sticking a thumb in his mouth.

'It's a funny hat isn't it, Loll? Just like a pair of frilly knickers put on upside down.' Great Aunt Annie giggled. 'Everyone used to wear them caps in the old days, everyone in service.'

'What's that she's got?' Lawrence was as well-practised as Julia in spinning out bedtime and he'd turned back to Goosey Goosey Gander.

'It's a candlestick, chuck. In the olden days, when there was no electricity . . .'

'Good *night*, Aunt Annie,' Mrs Bostock said firmly, shooing Loll up the stairs. She didn't want him falling asleep thinking about candles and striking matches.

That night she put a spare mattress on Julia's floor and he slept on it. The strong scorching, burning smell had evaporated as quickly as it had come but unless there was a fire in the town there was obviously some problem with the electrics in this old house, and that was dangerous. In the morning she'd ask Mrs Watkins over at the Vicarage for the name of an electrician. The wiring ought to be inspected for faults.

When Loll was asleep she went downstairs one last time to check round. As she climbed back upstairs the great black horse loomed up at her out of the darkness, stopping her in her tracks. There *was* a kind of coldness on this landing, but it was probably an ill-fitting window, or a damp wall. Even so, she shivered slightly as she stood there, thinking how Julia had grabbed at her hand.

The night it happened Mum and Dad were out at a special dinner in the Town Hall. Aunt Annie was 'baby-sitting', not that she had anything to do. Julia always put herself to bed and she got Loll organised too. They weren't *babies*.

At half past ten, just before she had her milky drink, Great Aunt Annie came all the way up to the top of the house to say good-night to them both. Julia was amazed. Surely she couldn't manage the steep attic stairs on those stumpy little legs of hers?

But she did. Julia heard 'Good night, chuck,' and Loll's door being pulled shut. Then there was a kind of heavy thud. She was puzzled. Great Aunt Annie was quite fat but it wasn't the repeated thudding of some-one lumbering down bare wooden stairs, just one big thud, then silence.

She forgot all about it in the embarrassment of the good-night kiss. The old lady waddled across the room and thrust a slightly prickly cheek up against Julia's. 'Night, night, chuck. Have you said your prayers?' She hadn't, of course, but if she confessed Aunt Annie might kneel down and start praying there and then.

'Good night, Auntie,' she said sleepily and ducked smartly under the covers, just in case another kiss was on its way.

The church clock woke her, St Christopher's on the other side of the square striking one. She sat up in bed and looked through the window. In the broad cobbled lane that ran along the backs of the houses there were spaces for people's cars but theirs was empty. Her parents must still be at the Town Hall.

She was trying to get back to sleep when she smelt the burning. She sat up again, pushed the window open and sniffed. It was a definite city smell, car fumes and factories and dogs, not fresh like the country. But there was no smell of fire. This smell was coming from *inside* the house, like the other times.

She ran into her parents' bedroom and switched on the light. Nothing amiss in here, just Mum's jeans hung neatly over a chair and Dad's clothes in a heap on the floor. He was messy like Loll. She and Mum were the two tidy ones.

Loll. Mum thought he was over his fire thing, but Julia wasn't so sure and she began to climb the attic stairs. Every single Friday he brought the Fireman book home from school. They all knew it off by heart. He was stuck on two things, that book and Goosey Goosey Gander in Aunt Annie's collection. His favourite picture was the girl in the knicker hat looking into dusty corners with her candlestick. 'My lady!' he shouted, whenever they got to that page.

When she reached the top of the stairs Julia stopped stone dead. Mum always left Loll's door open at night but Aunt Annie had closed it and now it wouldn't open again. She wrenched at the handle and pushed and kicked and yelled, but something heavy had fallen against the door from the inside. She hurled herself at it bodily, making it move a fraction of an inch, and through the crack smoke came curling, thick grey smoke that got thicker and darker by the second. 'Loll!' she screamed, then '*Lawrence!*' And through the crack she heard his voice, tight and high with terror, 'Julia!'

The nearest phone was in their kitchen. She almost fell down the attic steps then started on the main stairs. They were splintery and cold to her bare feet. As she reached the rocking horse landing she drew a deep breath. She'd never, ever, come as far down as this so late at night and, as she hurled herself past, the cold rushed out at her, just as if she'd opened a freezer cabinet. The flaring wooden nostrils of the great black wooden charger breathed winter, turning the inside air to ice.

As she picked up the kitchen phone she thought of that strange thud, just before Aunt Annie's whiskery good-night kiss. Now she knew what it was. The electricians were going to start rewiring next week and they'd been humping all the furniture about in the attics. Aunt Annie must have banged too hard when she shut the door. That wobbly old wardrobe must have fallen against it.

Julie heard herself telling the man on the other end of the phone that the fire was at 19 Baillie Square *and would they please hurry*. A child was trapped and she couldn't get the door open, and her aunt was old and her mum and dad still at the Town Hall. Her cool calm voice didn't sound a bit like her normal one. She felt separated from that cool-headed grown-up Julia by a thick wall of glass.

'*Julia!*' Loll's shrill scream of terror rang again in her ears.

'They'll be with you in a minute, love,' the man on the phone said calmly, *but a minute might be too late*. She scrabbled under the sink, found Dad's big hammer and made her way back upstairs. She'd once seen someone smash a door in with a hammer on TV. If she could make a big enough hole in one of the panels she could climb through and pull Loll out. He was only little.

She'd just reached the rocking horse landing when she heard a voice in the hall. 'Auntie Annie's gone to sleep,' it said blearily. 'You read it to me, Julia, I want to see my *lady*.' She spun round and almost fell back down the stairs. Lawrence was standing on the black and white tiles, his eyes still gummed up as if he'd been roused from a very deep sleep, the old nursery rhyme book thrust out hopefully towards her.

She'd not even reached him when there was a great hammering on the front door. 'S'cuse me, love,' three firemen shoved past and pelted up the stairs. Outside they could see three more, uncoiling a flat white hose, and a ladder was being unfolded in gleaming sections and propped against the house. Loll dropped his book and crept out on to the front door step, his eyes shining. 'Now then, back inside, little feller, you'll catch your death out here,' and a policeman was sweeping him up in his arms and carrying him into the kitchen.

Quite suddenly, Mum and Dad were there too. Mum had her arms round Julia, telling her she was a brave sensible girl who deserved a medal. Dad, who'd been down to check on Aunt Annie and found her peacefully asleep, was asking the firemen what was happening upstairs. Mum had forbidden him to go rushing about, because of his illness.

'Panic over,' someone said a few minutes later, coming downstairs. 'Sorry about all the water, sir. It always makes the biggest mess.' His hands and face were black and he'd left big splodgy footprints all over the bare boards. 'The blaze is out anyhow. It was in the eaves cupboard, just a load of old newspapers. Must have been there for years, from the look of them.'

'How did it happen, though?' Mum said. She wanted to cuddle Loll but he seemed quite happy with the policeman.

'Old wiring, from the look of it. It all needs ripping out, I'd say. Half the house fires we get are electrical. Good job there was nobody sleeping in that room. An old wardrobe had fallen against the door. It could have been a death trap.'

'But someone does sleep in there. Loll, our little boy . . . .'

'He'd gone down to see Aunt Annie as usual,' Julia said firmly. 'He wasn't there when the fire started.'

But he was. She'd heard him screaming on the other side of the door. How on earth had he escaped from that blazing attic? She'd not seen him slip past.

'It was the *lady*,' Lawrence said sleepily, finding Goosey Gander in his book, to show the policeman. 'She took me to see Aunt Annie, she takes me lots of nights. But Auntie was asleep,' he added reproachfully, 'and I've not had my sweet.'

Dad was sitting on a kitchen stool with Julia on his knee. Now the fire was out and Loll was safe she'd started to shiver. 'Your feet are cold,' her father said, chafing them with his big comforting hands. 'No wonder, walking up and down those stairs. I really must give the carpet people another ring, you've got some nasty splinters. And I'm getting another electrical firm in tomorrow, Mary. Harrisons should never have left the attic in that state. I feel like suing them.'

'This little chap's as warm as toast,' the policeman said suddenly. '*His* feet aren't cold, and I can't see any splinters. Funny that, when he's been running up and down the bare boards,' and he handed him back to his mother. It was true, Loll's feet felt like two tiny hot water bottles all pink and clean from his bath, not grimy and grey like Julia's. It was just as if someone had scooped him up from his bed, before the fire took hold, and carried him gently down to safety, so gently he'd hardly woken up.

As the last of the firemen shut the front door something rolled into a corner. Julia, who was wide awake now and looking forward to milk and biscuits before she went back to bed, bent down and picked it up. 'Where's this come from?' she said, taking the old bent candlestick and putting it on the kitchen table. Her mother shrugged. 'I don't know. I've never seen it before. Perhaps Aunt Annie put it out for St Christopher's jumble sale last week. I could polish that up. It's brass.'

Before the new electricians did the rewiring the attics were cleared out completely. Lawrence slept with Julia and although he'd loved his tiny room under the roof he didn't argue. It was all black now and it had a horrid burny smell still. The lady didn't like it either. She never came to see him any more, or carried him down to Aunt Annie.

The fireman had dumped the old newspapers in the middle of the floor and hosed them down. Dad, anxious to rescue what he could, went through the remains very carefully. Old papers fascinated him, and these were all local.

One rainy Sunday afternoon he looked up from the kitchen table, where he'd been piecing them together, and handed something to Mum. 'Read that,' he said, and his voice was strangely excited. Mum fished in her handbag for her glasses but Julia was already staring at the old yellow newspaper. At the top it said in Gothic capitals '**Darnley-in-Makerfield Examiner**, 27th March, 1888,' and underneath she read the headline

Coroner Warns about the Dangers of Reading in Bed

Sir Austen Greenald, Coroner for North West Lancashire, warned yesterday of

the dangers of lighted candles in confined
spaces. He was presiding at the inquest
on Jane Heslop, chamber maid of 19
Baillie Square, Darnley. The court listened to his summing up in which he
conjectured that the deceased, described
by her employer, Mr Albert Birdsall, as
'a most dutiful and honest girl, and one
anxious to extend her education' must
have been reading late at night and,
exhausted by her day's labours, fallen
asleep, letting her lighted candle drop to
the ground. Bedding, drapery and mat-
ting were all consumed and it is thought
that the deceased, overcome by smoke
before she could reach door or window,
died of suffocation.'

'27th March,' Dad said quietly. 'That was the day we
went to the Town Hall.'

'Oh yes,' Aunt Annie said when they showed her the
newspaper. 'Poor little Janey Heslop. She was a right
marvel she was, my mam told me all about her, up every
morning at four, carrying hot water cans, black-leading
all the grates, washing them tiles down. No wonder she
fell asleep at her books, poor little mite, she were only
fourteen. My dad gave her a proper funeral apparently,
horses and all. She hadn't got no family. They put her
little coffin up on the first landing, so folk could come
and pay their respects. There wasn't room in the hall,
it's that narrow. Oh aye, my mam told me all about
little Janey Heslop. They never let servants sleep in
them attics after. Then my father had the gas put in.'

The Bostocks stayed on at Aunt Annie's and Julia got
to like living in Baillie Square. She got to like her new

friends and her new school. She even got to like the house. They had a deep red carpet laid on the stairs and that awful cold feeling by the rocking horse never came again. Great Aunt Annie said it was because poor Janey was at peace now, she'd just had to 'stay on for a bit', till Loll was safe. They'd said a little prayer for Janey one night, after his story and his sweet, because she didn't come to see him any more and he missed her.

Six months after the fire Julia got a medal and a special certificate from something called The Royal Humane Society, because she'd been so brave on the night it happened. Loll was a bit jealous, soldiers had medals and this one was very big and shiny.

Still, he'd got his candlestick and that was shiny too now. Mum put it on his bookshelf with all his very special things and when he got frightened in the dark he switched his light on and looked at it for a minute. It reminded him of the lady.

The story of the servant girl who died while reading in bed is true. The original story appeared in the *Oxford Times* a hundred years ago. She lived in St John Street.

Rhodri Jones

I was born in the village of Gyffin, near Conway in North Wales, in 1933. The date on my birth certificate is 18th May, though I was actually born the day after – my father got the date wrong when he registered me!

My father was Welsh and my mother English, and I was the youngest of four sons. When I was two, the family moved to Troon on the west coast of Scotland where I spent twenty years. I think of myself as Scottish rather than Welsh.

I was educated at the local school – Marr College which was built by a successful businessman for all the children of the town. It must have been one of the first comprehensive schools. I went on to study English at Glasgow University. Then after two years' National Service in the Royal Navy, I began teaching in London.

As well as teaching, I wrote English textbooks for schools. I started writing novels only fairly recently – my first one, Delroy is Here, was published in 1983. I was headteacher of a North London multi-racial comprehensive school for eight years, and now I write full time.

Maybe it is my mixed Welsh/English/Scottish background which accounts for the pleasure I find in the richness of our multi-cultural society today. It may help me too to understand some of the difficulties minorities face through racism and prejudice. I remember when I was five or six being taunted at school for being Welsh – not much, but enough to make me cry. So Far to Go makes use of my Scottish memories, but most of my novels – Delroy is Here, Hillsden Riots, Getting it Wrong, Different Friends – are based on the experiences of some of my black pupils.

Recently, when I visited a school to talk about my books, a girl said to me afterwards, 'I hope you don't mind, but when I read The Private World of Leroy Brown, I thought you were black.' I didn't mind at all. I took it as a great compliment.

Leroy Brown is one of my favourite characters, so I thought you might enjoy another story about him and his friend Calamity.

No Pets Allowed

'Pete's 'ad some more babies,' Paulette announced at breakfast one morning.

'Oh, yes,' said Mum grimly. ''E sure do keep at it.'

Leroy studied his younger sister with a kind of bored fascination as he crunched his cornflakes. Pete, who lived in Paulette's classroom at school, gave birth with monotonous regularity, although the mystery of how a hamster with a name like that could have babies had never been satisfactorily explained.

'Mum,' Paulette went on, half hesitant, half pleading.

Leroy became more alert. From the way Paulette spoke, it was clear that she wanted something. He could tell.

'Yes?' Mum said, drawing the word out long and slow, and raising it in a question mark of suspicion. She must have noticed something in Paulette's voice as well.

Paulette took in a gulp of air and rushed on. 'Miss Pringle, she says she want the babies to go to good 'omes when they's old enough – an' Nicole an' Benny an' Sarah, they all says they gonna 'ave one – an', an' can I 'ave one too?'

There was a sudden silence as Paulette gazed hopefully up at Mum, and Mum stared back, a look of horror spreading across her face.

'A' 'amster!' Mum cried when she had recovered. 'We ain't 'avin' no 'amster in this 'ouse.'

'Aw, Mum.'

'They smells, don' they? An' chews t'ings up, don' they? Not to mention 'avin' babies all the time.'

'No, Mum,' Paulette protested. 'They's ever so clean, an' they's no trouble at all. You'd never know 'e was 'ere.'

'Don' seem much point in 'avin' 'im then.'

'Aw, Mum.'

'Anyways. It's against the rules. We ain't allowed no pets. That's what it say in the rent book.'

Paulette's eyes filled with reproachful tears.

'Ain't no use lookin' at me like that,' said Mum. 'I don' make up the rules. The boro' do.'

'It ain't fair,' mumbled Paulette, beginning to sulk.

'I knows it ain't fair,' agreed Mum. 'But life ain't fair. The sooner you learns that the better. Now where's that Floyd? 'E gonna be late for school again.'

She got up from the table and went to the door. 'Floyd,' she called warningly.

Leroy gulped down the remains of his tea. 'Come on, Paulette,' he said. It would be wiser to get off to school. He didn't want to be there when his brother finally emerged and the storm broke.

Paulette was silent, brooding over her disappointment all the way to school – along the walkway, down the five flights of stairs (the lifts were out of order as usual), through the shopping centre and along The Avenue.

It wasn't until they reached the gates of Beechcroft Junior School that she turned to Leroy and asked, 'Don' you t'ink it ain't fair? Wouldn' you like to 'ave a pet?'

'I ain't really t'ought 'bout it,' Leroy replied.

But as he continued up The Avenue, he did begin to think about it. Maybe it would be fun to have a pet.

Not a hamster, but a real pet. A dog, for instance. Now that would really be something.

But it would have to be the right kind of dog. An Alsatian perhaps. He'd seen them in the park – big, powerful, wolf-like; pink tongues lolling out and licking their lips; yellow eyes roving round like searchlights. A dog like that would be worth having.

Or there were those red dogs – setters, were they, or retrievers – with coats as dark and glossy as chestnuts that advertised dogfood on television. They certainly had style. He wouldn't mind being seen with one of them in the park, throwing sticks for it, calling it to heel, commanding its unswerving devotion and obedience.

But the idea was impossible. A dog like that would cost a fortune in tins of dog meat. It would probably eat more than he did, and he ate enough for two – at least so Mum kept telling him.

And then, it would need hours and hours of exercise – runs and chases and wide open spaces. You couldn't keep it cooped up all the time in a council flat.

And anyway, there were rules against it. The council wouldn't permit it. No pets allowed.

His dream knocked on the head, Leroy sighed and returned to the business of getting to school. He raised his eyes to check for traffic before crossing the road, and then lowered them to the pavement at his feet. He blinked, looked away and then looked back again to make sure he was seeing right.

Gazing up at him was a dog. It wasn't anything like the dogs he had been thinking about. It was small, sandy-brown in colour, with short tight hair. It had a sharp pointed head, thin spindly legs and a tail with a curl in it. Leroy couldn't imagine what breed it was. Or whether it belonged to any breed at all.

The dog had its head cocked to one side. Its bright black eyes were fixed on him, and its mouth was stretched wide showing its teeth. It looked as though it was grinning up at him. He wasn't sure if dogs did grin, but that was what it looked like.

He bent down to pat the dog on the head and said, 'Good dog.' That seemed to be what the dog wanted him to do. It responded by pushing its head against Leroy's hand and wagging its tail, though the curl didn't unwind. It ran its tongue over its nose and lips and then gazed up at him again with its mouth arranged once more in an idiotic grin.

That's enough of that, Leroy thought. There was a gap in the traffic, and he crossed the road.

When he reached the other side, he was surprised to find that the dog was still with him – head at an angle, eyes moist and shining, mouth gaping wide as before.

For a moment, Leroy felt a touch of exasperation. What was the dog up to? It wasn't following him, was it? But then it dawned on him that the dog was simply being sensible. It had been waiting until it was safe to cross the road and had used Leroy as a guide. It was the sort of thing old ladies used boy scouts for.

Pleased that he had done his good deed for the day, Leroy patted the dog on the head once more and set off towards the school gates.

He had only gone a few paces when he realised that the dog was trotting along beside him, its head on one side, looking up at him happily. It was a wonder it could see where it was going.

Leroy gave a grunt of annoyance. Why did the dog have to attach itself to him? There were lots of other people hurrying by on their way to school. It could have chosen any one of them. It was embarrassing. He didn't want to be seen with this miserable mongrel hanging on to him like this – though 'miserable' was hardly the right word. The dog was still grinning away fit to get lockjaw.

'Go 'way,' Leroy muttered at it between clenched teeth, hoping no one would hear or see.

But the dog might as well have been deaf for all the notice it took. Leroy decided the best thing would be simply to ignore it, pretend it wasn't there. That way the dog would soon get tired and go away.

Keeping his head up and his eyes forward, he marched on.

Calamity was waiting for him at the school gates. 'Hi,' his friend greeted him. 'Have you done – '

Calamity broke off. Leroy knew he was asking him if he had done his homework. Calamity always wanted to copy it. But somehow the words had stuck in his throat. He was staring down at the pavement with a puzzled look on his face. Leroy followed his gaze. That wretched dog was still there, raising its eyes adoringly and grinning as ever.

Calamity found his voice. 'I never knew you 'ad a dog.'

'I ain't,' Leroy snapped.

'Who's your friend then?'

'I dunno do I? 'E jus' latch on to me.'

'Must be your irresistible charm,' said Calamity, and he began to grin too.

'Don' you start,' Leroy warned. 'Let's get goin'.' The sooner they were inside the school grounds the better. The dog wouldn't follow him there.

But it did. Its thin legs going up and down like

pistons, it kept pace with Leroy and Calamity as they hurried up the drive. Crowds of other pupils were also making for the main building, but the dog only had eyes for Leroy.

''E's still there,' Calamity informed him.

Leroy squinted down at the dog with distaste and quickly averted his eyes.

''E really do seem to fancy you,' Calamity went on, trying not to laugh.

Leroy pressed his lips firmly together and ignored him.

Skipping to the other side of Leroy, Calamity bent down and rubbed the dog's head. 'Who's a good boy then?' he crooned.

Leroy clicked his tongue against his teeth. 'Don' encourage 'im.'

But the dog wasn't interested in Calamity. A quick flick of his eyes was all it gave him before returning to fix Leroy once more with its grimace of delighted devotion.

'What you gonna do?' Calamity asked. 'You can't 'ave that thing trottin' round with you all day. The teachers won't let you.'

Leroy controlled himself. As if he didn't know that. But then he sneaked a quick glance at his friend. Calamity's face looked innocent enough, though you couldn't always tell. A nagging suspicion began to grow. Could it be that Calamity was enjoying the situation?

'Ain't my fault,' he muttered irritably, though he knew that wouldn't help him if there was trouble.

'The teachers ain't gonna say that,' Calamity said, echoing his thoughts.

Leroy didn't bother to reply. Calamity was a real ray

of sunshine and no mistake. Pretend it's not there. That was the only answer, Leroy told himself once more.

By now, they had reached the top playground. For once, the senior boys hadn't taken it over for their mad game of shin-kicking. They were probably all in the toilets smoking themselves to death. The first-year boys had the playground to themselves and were chasing a tennis ball from one side of the asphalt to the other.

'Come on,' Leroy called out to Calamity as he threw his case down and charged on to the playground to lose himself in the crowd. It was one way of getting away from that dog. It would never be able to find him in that surging, seething mob.

He raced towards the ball, dodging this way and that as he passed player after player. Lalji had just kicked the ball. It was skimming over the ground. Leroy stuck out a foot and trapped it. He made a swift survey of the field to see where people were positioned. Then he swung his leg back ready to boot the ball towards the goal.

That was when he heard it. 'Woof, woof.' That was exactly what it sounded like. 'Woof, woof' – loud and high and getting nearer.

Leroy looked round, and there was the dog hurling itself across the playground towards him. When it reached him, it skidded to a halt. It sniffed at the ball and said, 'Woof, woof,' again. As it did so, it blinked its eyes violently and shook its head like somebody trying to cough up a fish bone or something stuck in his throat. Leroy had time to feel amazed that such a small dog could make so much noise. Close to, it was ear-shattering.

Having announced its arrival, the dog wagged its tail

as best it could with that curl in it, and gazed up at Leroy, full of pleasure at having found him again.

Leroy decided to play on. He gave the ball a good kick and set off to follow it.

'Woof, woof,' went the dog as it chased at his heels. It seemed to think it was some new kind of game specially put on for its benefit. Leroy found himself tripping over his own feet as he tried to prevent himself from stepping on the dog. The dog grinned up at him happily.

At last he just gave up. The others were giving up too.

'What's that dog doing here?' someone wanted to know.

'Clear off,' others yelled.

Several boys made threatening gestures at the dog to try to drive it away. But it took no notice. As far as it was concerned, there was only one person there.

Before they could carry on with the game, the hooter sounded for the beginning of school. Amidst grumbles and moans, shouts and shrieks, everyone went to collect bags and blazers and line up. In the crush and confusion, Leroy lost sight of the dog. He breathed a sigh of relief. He'd got rid of it at last. He hurried to join the rest of the pupils in 1B.

Mr Garfield came out of the school building with his gown wrapped round him and mounted the steps to the playground to inspect the troops before they went into school. Slowly he went up and down the ranks of pupils, his fierce eye searching for glints of jewellery and banned badges and fluorescent socks.

He was just approaching 1B when Leroy heard Calamity whisper behind him, ''E's still 'ere.'

Leroy groaned. He looked down, and there sure

enough was the dog, head on one side, eyes raised, delighted to reclaim his acquaintance. There was nothing Leroy could do but wait, though he kept his gaze well clear of Mr Garfield as a precaution.

The deputy head's voice broke through the silence. 'What is this I see before me?' From the way he spoke, Leroy suspected that he knew perfectly well what it was.

Nobody else said anything. Leroy snatched a quick glance at Mr Garfield and the dog. Mr Garfield was staring grimly at the dog, and the dog had turned its head briefly to see who had made the noise before returning to direct its admiration at Leroy. Who needed enemies when you had friends like that, Leroy thought glumly, as he tried to shrink into insignificance. The dog's eyes gazing up at him were as bad as an accusing finger.

It didn't need Veronica Wright to state the obvious, but she spoke up anyway, the way she always did.

'I think it's Leroy Brown's, sir,' she said smugly.

'Brown,' Mr Garfield thundered, and Leroy was forced to look at him. 'Does this animal belong to you?'

'No, sir,' Leroy mumbled.

'Then why is it standing there with that love-sick expression on its face?'

Leroy heard a splutter behind him that was quickly suppressed.

'I dunno, sir,' he said, making a mental note to thump Calamity at his earliest convenience.

Mr Garfield pursed his lips and went, 'Hmmm.' The long drawn-out sound was heavy with doubt and suspicion. It was funny, Leroy had time to think, the way teachers never believed you when you told them the

the truth. If he had told a lie – said the dog was his – Mr Garfield would have accepted it without question.

'Well, it seems to have attached itself to you,' Mr Garfield said at last. 'Do something about it.'

'Sir?' Leroy asked. What on earth did Mr Garfield want him to do?

'Get rid of it.'

'But how, sir?'

'Take it down to the school gate and lose it.'

It was all very well for Mr Garfield to talk, Leroy thought grimly. He didn't know what the dog was like. He hadn't had it following at his heels for the last half hour.

But when Mr Garfield told you to do something, you didn't have much option. Reluctantly, Leroy stepped out of line. He scowled down at the dog and set off across the playground. Behind him, he could hear people laughing and tittering and Mr Garfield calling, 'Make a good job of it. We can't have dogs running wild all over the school.'

Leroy scowled again at the miserable specimen trotting along beside him. If only it had run wild. Then he wouldn't have been landed in this hole.

There was no problem about getting the dog to the front gate. It padded down the drive with him, the picture of contented loyalty. It was at the front gate that Leroy found himself at a loss.

He tried walking out on to the pavement and then coming back through the gate. But the dog just followed him.

He tried shooing the dog away, waving his hands at it and shouting, 'Get off. Scram.' But the dog didn't move.

He tried pointing up the road and crying eagerly, 'Look. There you are. Go on.' But the dog merely blinked blankly in the direction indicated and stayed where it was.

By now, Leroy was fuming. What had he done to deserve this, he demanded to know. He leaned over the low wall of the garden next to the school and picked up a stone. It would serve that wretched animal right if he threw it at it. But the dog had such a happy trustful look on its face that Leroy couldn't bring himself to do it.

Instead, he hurled the stone along the pavement and yelled, 'Go get.'

They both watched as the stone went bouncing and skittering into the distance. The dog continued to watch as the stone narrowly missed a woman on her way to the shopping centre. She gave a leap in the air, wheeled round and began mouthing words at them. But Leroy didn't hear or see them. He had cringed back and was hiding his head in his hands.

'Now look what you've done,' he muttered at the dog. But the dog didn't seem at all concerned or repentant. It just grinned up at him as brightly as ever.

Leroy was growing desperate. What else could he do? Wherever he went, the dog seemed determined to follow. It could have given Mary's little lamb a lesson or two. If only he could tie it to something. The dog had a collar. It would be possible to slip a piece of rope or string through that and tie it to the railing at the side of the gate. But he didn't have any rope or string. All he had that was suitable was the belt holding up his trousers, and he didn't feel like sacrificing that. Apart from anything else, there was what Mum would have to say if he arrived home without it.

But it had given him an idea. The collar. Of course. Why hadn't he thought of it before? Eagerly, he bent down and pulled the collar round to see if there was a tag on it. The dog didn't seem to mind, and yes, there was, a thin metal disc with words punched into it. 'Tiger' – that must be the dog's name. (Tiger! It had to be someone's idea of a joke.) And then there was an address – '25 The Avenue'. But he was standing in The Avenue now. Number 25 was at the other end near the shopping centre. All he had to do was take the dog there, and his problem was solved.

Feeling light-headed with relief, Leroy straightened up. He began to smile and congratulate himself on his powers of deduction. Maybe he should become a detective when he grew up. He clearly had a talent for it.

And then suddenly his thoughts were interrupted.

'What are you doing with my dog?' a voice demanded close behind him.

Leroy spun round and found himself face to face with a man a few inches away from him. The man's face was tight and threatening. Leroy began to grow worried, but he was indignant too.

'I ain't doin' not'in',' he retorted.

'You're trying to steal him, aren't you?' the man accused.

Leroy couldn't believe it. Steal! He'd have gladly given the beast away to anyone who would take it.

'I've heard of people like you,' the man went on furiously. 'You pick up dogs off the street and take them home and keep them. Or' – another idea struck him – 'you sell them to those firms that make cat meat.'

Leroy was incensed. As if he'd do a thing like that – either of them.

'I weren't tryin' to steal you' dog. In fact, I were tryin' to get rid o' 'im. 'E follow me into school, an' I were jus' takin' 'im back to 'is 'ome. 25 The Avenue, innit?'

The fierce expression on the man's face began to falter. 'Yes, that's right.'

Leroy pressed his advantage. 'You ask Mr Garfield if you don' believe me. 'E's the deputy 'ead.'

By now, the man's anger had collapsed completely. 'I'm sorry . . .' he stammered. 'I didn't realise . . . Here.'

He dug his hand into his trousers' pocket and brought out a handful of change. He selected two pound coins and pressed them into Leroy's palm.

'Thanks,' he said apologetically. 'Sorry I accused you. I'm really very grateful.'

'Thank you,' Leroy managed to splutter when he had recovered from his surprise.

All this time, the dog had been standing quietly. The man took a lead out of his coat pocket and attached it to the dog's collar. Leroy was disconcerted to see that the dog was gazing up at the man with the grin and the adoring eyes that had previously been reserved for him. It didn't look at Leroy at all. He felt a twinge of disappointment. There's gratitude for you, he thought. How fickle can you get?

'I'll take him off home then,' the man said. 'Thanks again.'

'That's OK,' Leroy said.

He watched as the man walked away down The Avenue with the dog trotting at his side, its head at an angle gazing upwards. But no matter how long Leroy watched, the dog didn't look back once.

Slowly he turned and went back through the school gates. He was going to be late for his first lesson, but that was all right. There was no need to hurry. He had a good excuse.

As he trudged up the drive, he thought again about Paulette's question earlier that morning. Would he like to have a pet? Maybe yes, maybe no. They could have their drawbacks. But probably, on the whole, they were a good thing – especially if they belonged to other people.

And he happily jingled the pound coins in his pocket.

Joan Lingard

I was born in a taxi cab in the Royal Mile of Edinburgh. I've always been pleased about that since the taxi suggests mobility and movement and the Royal Mile, which runs from the castle down to Holyrood Palace, tradition and the past.

At the age of two I went to live in Belfast, where I stayed until I was eighteen, and so did all my growing up there. It was where I went to school, and began to read and to write.

As a child I was absolutely crazy about books. I read everything that I could get my hands on, from Enid Blyton to Little Women, *from the Chalet School books to* Just William, Pollyanna *and* Biggles. *Everything that was in my local children's library, in fact. One day when I was eleven years old and had nothing to read and was moaning in my mother's ear about how bored I was, she turned round and said: 'Why don't you go and write a book of your own?' Why not indeed? So I took lined, foolscap paper, filled my fountain pen with green ink and began. My first novel was set in Cornwall – where I'd never been. All my early writing was set in places where I'd never set foot in but as I grew older I realised that I'd write more convincingly if I wrote about places and people that I knew and understood.*

And so it has proved. From my Belfast childhood have come my Kevin *and* Sadie *books and* The File on Fräulein Berg, *also Josie, the heroine of* The Guilty Party, *and one of the strands of* The Winter Visitor.

Many of my other books such as the Maggie *quartet,* The Gooseberry *and* Rags and Riches *have come from the Scottish side of my life for at eighteen I returned to Edinburgh, the city of my birth, where I now live.*

Bicycle Thieves

'Why should *I* have to have her in *my* room?' demanded Tamsy, stamping up and down the kitchen floor. 'Why can't Emily? She's nearer Emily's age. It's not fair!'

'I have to study,' said Emily, who was reading *Jackie* magazine. 'I need peace and quiet.'

'You, study?' said Ben. He was blacking his rugby boots. 'That'll be the day.'

Emily picked up the telephone directory from the numerous objects available on the table and threw it at him. She missed, hitting instead the cactus plant on the window sill. It toppled to the floor spilling its soil.

'Better get that cleaned up before your mother comes back,' said Henry, glancing up from his book. Henry was their father. Emily did not get up. 'Move!' he said.

Grumbling, she took a spoon from the drawer and began to scrape up the soil from the floor. 'It looks half dead, anyway.'

'Daddy, why *do* I have to have her in my room?' Tamsy put her hand on his shoulder.

'Listen to Little Miss Simper,' said Emily. 'She can't half turn it on.'

Tamsy stuck her tongue so far out that she thought she'd sprained it. She pulled it back in and sucked her cheeks together.

'You're all being horrible,' said Henry mildly. 'I'm

ashamed of you. You'll have to show a little Christian charity to the lass.'

'I don't know why you talk about Christian charity,' said Ben. 'When were you last in a church?'

Henry turned over a page of his book.

'You weren't keen on the idea, were you, Henry?' said Emily. 'Not when Mary first mentioned it.' Mary was their mother.

'Well, maybe not *keen* exactly. I feel I've got enough on my hands as it is with you lot. But what else could we do? She's the daughter of your mother's oldest friend. And, as you know, her mother asked your mother before she died if we'd take her.'

Her mother had said, 'I'd like Isla to be part of a warm, lively family.'

'We can't go back on a promise, can we?'

'I don't know why you say "we",' said Emily. 'I'm sure she'd have been much happier staying with someone on her island. I can't see her liking it here.'

The Dochertys lived in a large top floor flat in the centre of Edinburgh.

'There they are now,' said Ben.

He laid aside his boots; Emily dropped the cactus plant; Tamsy stood still, on one leg, as if she were playing statues; and Henry let his book slide down on to his lap.

They heard the flat door closing and Mary saying brightly, 'Here we are then, Isla. This is where we live. It's a bit of a climb up, isn't it, but you'll soon get used to it. I expect the family is in the kitchen – that's where we tend to live.' Mary was speaking too brightly.

She came into the kitchen, scouring it with her eyes to see if they had done all the things they were supposed to have done in her absence. (They hadn't. Ben had washed the dishes, though not the pots, and Emily hadn't got round to drying them. And Tamsy's homework jotter lay unopened on the table in the middle of a pile of comics, coloured crayons, socks, elastic bands, pictures cut from magazines for a project she was doing in school, a ball of wool that the cat had tangled, knitting needles, library books, screwed up chocolate wrappers, a brush full of Emily's hairs and a hair dryer, and Ben's rugby boots. Mary opened her mouth to deliver a blast then, remembering the girl who stood behind her, said, not quite as heartily as before:

'Isla, this is the family.' And she stood aside so that they could see the girl. She was tall for her age – twelve – and very pale and she had lank black hair held back from her narrow face by two bubblegum-pink clasps. She wore a navy-blue skirt and socks and a hand-knitted grey jersey.

Mary introduced each of them in turn. Henry jumped up at once and took her hand and said, 'Welcome to Edinburgh, Isla! We're very pleased that you've come to live with us.' Ben, Emily and Tamsy nodded and said, 'Hello' or 'Hi'. The girl said nothing. Her dark eyes roamed round the kitchen then came back to rest on the floor in front of her feet.

'Well now, I expect you're hungry?' Mary broke off to say, 'What have you been doing to my plant, Emily? And I've told you before that you are *not* to borrow my hair dryer without asking! And get those boots off the table, Ben! How many times do I have to tell you . . .?'

'All right, all right,' said Ben. 'No need to go lathering on.'

'I'll lather you!' Mary, remembering the girl again, subsided. But she gave Ben a meaningful look before turning back to the newcomer. 'Sit down, dear, and we'll get you some supper. We've kept you something in the oven. Clear this table, Tamsy! *At once*! It looks as if you've tipped the entire contents of your schoolbag over it.'

'It's not all my stuff!'

'Stop arguing! Here you are, dear, have this chair.' Mary removed a pile of tee-shirts and jeans which were waiting to be ironed and transferred them to the formica working-top beside the bread bin. 'Emily, get Isla's supper from the oven. Would you like some juice, Isla? Apple or orange?' Isla nodded. 'Apple?' asked Mary. Isla nodded.

Mary took the packet from the fridge. She shook it.

'Who put this empty packet back in the fridge?'

'Not me,' said Tamsy.

'It's always not me. That mysterious person. Isla, do you know someone whose name is Not Me?' Mary laughed, but Isla stared blankly back. 'It'll have to be orange juice then. Do you like orange?'

Isla nodded.

Supper, a dish of aubergines, peppers and courgettes, cooked with tomatoes in a casserole, and topped with cheese, looked somewhat shrivelled and dried.

'Oh dear!' said Mary. 'Sorry about that, Isla. But your bus was very late, wasn't it? I hope you like aubergines?'

Isla neither nodded nor shook her head. She fiddled about amongst the food with her knife and fork, eating very little, and drank half a glass of orange juice. Henry talked to her about her journey, or tried to, but she did not respond.

Mary said, 'Why haven't you done your homework yet, Tamsy? Henry, why didn't you see she did her homework?'

'You know I don't approve of homework for nine year olds.'

Isla's eyes swivelled from one to the other.

'It's only half a dozen spellings, for goodness sake! It won't kill her to do that every night. She's a rotten speller, anyway.' Mary ignored Tamsy's protests. 'Are you good at spelling, Isla?' she asked.

As they were now coming to expect, Isla did not answer. Mary was looking exhausted. Emily began to dry the dishes.

'By the way,' said Mary, 'I didn't see your bicycle down there when we came in, Ben.'

'You didn't?' He shot out of the room.

'Don't tell me it's been pinched again,' said Emily. 'Those bicycle thieves are the limit!'

'They're horrible, those thieves,' Tamsy said to Isla. 'I left my bike outside for just two minutes while I ran up to get my anorak and when I went back down it was gone. They stand round the corner watching you and they wear balaclava helmets pulled down over their faces.'

Isla's black eyes grew large with alarm.

'Don't tell lies, Tamsy,' said her mother. 'You've never seen anyone in a balaclava helmet standing round the corner.'

'They could wear them. How do you know they don't?'

'But you know you can't leave your bikes even for two minutes without chaining them up,' said Henry.

'The thieves tour round in vans lifting bikes,' Emily explained to Isla, 'and then they take them apart in secret workshops and re-assemble them and change the numbers and sell them again.'

'Do you have bicycle thieves on your island?' asked Tamsy.

'Don't be silly,' said Emily. 'The police could easily track them down on an island.'

Ben came bursting into the room, his face red with fury. 'It's gone! My new bike! If I could lay my hands on them . . .' He held a severed chain. 'They cut the chain.' He threw it angrily on to the floor.

'That won't help.' Henry sighed. 'I'll have to get on to the insurance, *again*. I don't know what they're going to say. Last time they were suspicious enough. "You seem to lose an awful lot of bicycles in your family, Mr Docherty," they said.'

'You'll have to bring your bike up the stairs in future,' said Mary. 'We've told you before.'

'I was going to go out again to see Jim. It's a heck of a long way to carry it up and down *every* time.'

'Emily carried hers up.'

Emily smirked.

Isla's head was drooping over her plate.

'Come on, dear,' said Mary, helping her up. 'It's been a long day for you. And you, too, Tamsy, and don't start giving me all that about having homework to do – it's too late now. It'll serve you right if you get a row from your teacher.'

When she came back, on her own, she sank down into a chair.

'I've been telling these two not to lay it on too thick about bicycle thieves,' said Henry. 'The poor lass'll probably dream about them. She'll be thinking the town's a terrible place.'

'It's not us that lays it on thick,' objected Emily. 'It's that wee squirt of a sister.'

'That's no way to talk about your sister!' Mary looked

at Emily and Ben. 'You will have to make an effort with Isla! You've got to remember she's going through a very difficult time.'

'What can we do if she won't speak?' said Emily.

'Maybe she can't speak,' suggested Ben.

'She said hello to me when I met her off the bus.'

'So are you trying to say that it's us that have struck her dumb?' asked Emily.

'It's perfectly possible,' said their mother.

'If she would even cry!' said Mary.

They were having one of their interminable discussions about what-to-do-about-Isla. Ben said they were interminable because they went on and on until it was time to go bed and they never came to any conclusion. Isla and Tamsy were already in bed, or supposed to be. The bumps they could hear suggested that Tamsy was practising handsprings.

Isla had been with them for a month, and during that time had not said one word that anyone had heard, except for 'Hello' when Mary had met her off the bus. The headmaster and teachers at school were being very understanding and while they spoke to her they did not press her to speak in return. The guidance teacher had had two or three sessions with her and said all the things she might be expected to say like, 'I expect you're missing your mother very much. I expect you're missing your island very much. I expect you're finding it very difficult to settle down with a new family. I expect you're finding the city strange.' The educational psychologist had two sessions with her, also, and had said much the same things. But no matter what anyone said, Isla said nothing. She might at times nod or shake her head or lift her shoulders in a slight shrug but often the expression on her face did not change at all. She set off for school with Ben and Emily in the mornings and went inside the building but at the first opportunity slipped away.

Where she went, they did not know. Both Mary and Henry were out working all day – Mary was a chemical engineer, Henry a librarian – and neither could come out of work to go chasing her.

'I'm sure she just walks round the streets,' said Emily. One of her friends had seen her when she'd been off school sick and Emily had seen her herself one day on the way to the museum on a school trip. Isla had not seen her. Isla had been walking along the other side of the road with her head bent down, looking into the basement flats. They saw her walking on their own street, staring with her great big black eyes into the basements. It was as if she could not understand how people lived below the level of the road.

She also stood at the window of her bedroom – hers and Tamsy's – and stared at the high grey block of flats across the street. Mary had tried to point out that city-scapes had their own charm, with their different heights of roofs and different shaped chimney pots, and church spires and towers sticking up. And wasn't the sky beautiful when the sun was setting above the rooftops? She and Henry took her for walks in the Botanic Garden and through the Queen's Park and along the foreshore at Cramond though, perhaps, Mary said, that was not such a good idea as the sight of the sea might make her feel more homesick. Henry thought it would be better if she did feel homesick, or at least if she would express it.

Tamsy hated seeing Isla standing at the bedroom

window staring out. It made her feel funny, she complained. She wanted to move in with Emily but Emily said no deal, she liked to have her friends in and she didn't want *her* around listening to their conversation. Tamsy said it wasn't fair, she couldn't have her best friend Helen to stay overnight any more. She said she hated being the youngest in the family. She said they were a horrible family. Henry said they would all have to stop arguing.

'The psychologist says she needs time,' said Mary, 'and lots of affection.'

'How can you be affectionate to a stone wall?' asked Emily.

'Don't be so heartless! You should feel sorry for her.'

'I do feel sorry for her. And you don't have to tell me what to feel!' Emily got up and left the room, slamming the door behind her.

'She's impossible at the moment. If you as much as look at her the wrong way she flies up in the air like a kite.'

'It's her age,' said Ben. And grinned. He was feeling cheerful as the insurance money had just come through and he was going to go round the bicycle shops the next day to look for a new one.

But before he got the chance to do that, another family cycle went missing. When Henry opened the door to the postman in the morning, he found that Emily's bicycle had gone. She had left it on the top landing the night before, chained to the railing.

'I'm sure I did, I definitely did. You saw it, Ben, didn't you?' He confirmed that he had.

Someone coming home late in the evening must have neglected to shut the bottom door properly, in spite of the fact that Ben had put up a notice printed in red saying 'Bicycle thieves operating. Please make sure the door is securely shut.' The flat beneath theirs was occupied by five students who came and went at all hours and were not at all careful about shutting the door, and who didn't wash the stairs, either, when it was their turn. Mary was forever chasing after them about it.

The family gathered on the landing in their dressing-gowns to stare at the black iron railings to which the bicycle had been tethered.

'It's terrible, isn't it, dear?' said Mary, turning to Isla, who had just appeared in the doorway.

Isla nodded.

It was the same evening, and Tamsy was sitting up in bed crayoning a picture of bicycle thieves with black balaclava helmets pulled down over their faces. At least it meant she didn't have to draw faces. She wasn't very good at them. Isla was standing, as usual, at the window. She had been there for ages.

'What can you see there?' asked Tamsy and leaping out of bed, went to join her at the window.

The street was lined with parked cars, vans and motor bikes on either side; it always was. Mary and Henry complained about not being able to find a space for their car even though they paid for residential parking. On Isla's island there would be very few cars, Tamsy supposed. Isla had lived in a hamlet of six cottages and had known everyone, which had its advantages and disadvantages, Mary said. It was friendly but, on the other hand, you never had any privacy.

'You'll get used to it, you know,' said Tamsy. 'Once you make some friends you'll like it better.'

Isla did not answer. Tamsy was getting used to that

and didn't let it stop her talking. She went back to bed and to her drawing.

'I'm not very good at drawing bicycles. I can't seem to make the wheels proper circles.'

'Bicycle thieves!' cried Isla suddenly, and Tamsy nearly fell out of bed with shock.

She went rushing through to the kitchen shouting, 'Isla's spoken! Isla's *spoken!*'

'What did she say?' asked Henry.

'Bicycle thieves.'

They ran through to the bedroom. Isla was still standing by the window; she was trembling and clutching her hands together in front of her with excitement.

'Bicycle thieves,' she said.

'That's fantastic,' said Emily.

Henry put his arm round Isla's shoulder and asked her gently, 'Did you *see* bicycle thieves?'

She nodded.

'Say yes or no.'

'Yes.'

'Where?'

She pointed across the road to where a blue van stood parked. 'Over there.'

'In the van?'

'No, the basement. Two boys went down the steps with bicycles.'

'But they might be their own bicycles, Henry,' said Ben.

'I've seen them before,' said Isla. 'With other bicycles.'

'I suppose we'd better phone the police,' said Mary, sounding unsure. 'Just in case.'

Henry made the call and the girls got dressed. Then

they all went down the stairs and waited on the pavement.

Two police cars entered the street within five minutes and as they drew up the lights went off in the basement across the road. The Dochertys and Isla crossed over.

'There's someone in,' Henry told the sergeant.

The sergeant and one of the constables went down the steps and banged on the door, the other two policemen remained on the pavement.

'Open up! We know there's someone in.'

The door opened and a middle-aged man, whom the Dochertys had seen going up and down the street, looked out. He was wearing a brown cardigan and glasses. He didn't look like a bicycle thief.

'I was just going to bed,' he protested. 'I've had flu.'

'If you don't mind we'd like a word with you?' said the sergeant. They went inside.

They found twelve bicycles all dismantled and done up in brown sacks. The sacks would then have been put into the blue van which was parked outside and driven off to a garage. The man was a bicycle receiver. And the two youths found hiding behind the dustbins in the back yard were bicycle thieves. They were brought up the steps, along with the receiver, their wrists handcuffed, and bundled into the police cars. The youths were wearing jeans and anoraks. 'No balaclava helmets!' said Tamsy.

'A good piece of detection work, young lady,' the sergeant said to Isla. 'I'll come round tomorrow and take your statement.'

The police cars drove off. Isla burst into tears.

'There now, love, it's all right,' said Mary and put her arms round her. 'You've been marvellous. Let's all go upstairs and have some hot chocolate.'

'And chocolate biscuits?' said Tamsy.

They sat round the table drinking the hot chocolate.

'Imagine – they were across the road all the time!' said Ben. 'And it took Isla to come along and see them.'

'You were brill, Isla,' said Emily.

'Thank you,' said Isla. And smiled.

Terrance Dicks

I was born in London's East End just before World War Two and can still remember the air raids and evacuations that form the background to this story.

After the war we came back to London, and eventually the eleven-plus took me to Grammar School. From there, a scholarship took me to Cambridge and an English degree.

National Service swallowed up the next two years. I was stationed in the Tower of London, and could usually get home for tea.

After a few years as an advertising copywriter I eventually became a freelance scriptwriter, first in radio then in television.

Five years as script editor of Doctor Who *led to the writing of over fifty* Doctor Who *books, and these in turn led to about fifty other childrens' books, mostly for younger children.*

I later returned to the BBC, first as script editor and currently as producer of the BBC's Sunday Classic Serial.

Along the way I got married and subsequently acquired three sons, now all bigger than I am, a rickety book-filled house, a dog, two cats, two budgerigars, two goldfish, a rat, a mouse, a gerbil and a tortoise.

London's Burning

I was in bed, huddled under the blankets, fully dressed except for shoes. I was waiting for Mr Pinnock to go to bed and fall asleep.

I knew it wouldn't take long. Farmers get up early. They go to bed early too. Suddenly I heard Mr Pinnock climbing the stairs, booted feet thumping on the bare boards.

I heard his bedroom door open on the landing below, heard the groan of the bedsprings as he slumped down on the edge of the bed beside his wife. I heard a low rumble of conversation, his wheezes as he wrestled his way out of his clothes and into his nightshirt, the clonk of first one boot then the other hitting the floor.

I heard the squeak of the bedsprings as he climbed into bed.

More endless-seeming waiting – until at last I heard the rumble of his snores, blending in a sort of duet with those of his wife.

It was time to go.

I slipped out of bed. I took my shoes, laces already tied together, from under the bed and hung them round my neck.

I crept out of the little attic room and down the stairs. They creaked at every step as if determined to betray me.

I reached the landing. Holding my breath, I crept past

the Pinnocks' door, past the door of my enemy, Patrick, their son.

More stairs, then I was in the kitchen, still lit by the glow of the dying fire. The kitchen door was locked and bolted, the big key still in the lock. I turned it slowly, wincing at the final click which rang out like a shot. The rusty bolts were my next problem. I got some dripping from the meat tin on the stove and greased them with it, and they slid back quietly enough. I went out into the farmyard. It was warmer than I'd expected, and not too dark.

Prince, the black and white sheepdog was stretched out in front of his kennel. He lifted his head as I came out, but thank goodness he didn't bark. I bent down and patted his shaggy head. Prince was my only real friend at Pinnock's farm. I was tempted to take him with me, but I decided it would be stealing. I crossed the yard, climbed over the gate and dropped down into the lane. It was dark in the lane, but no darker than the black-out at home, and I knew more or less where I was going.

At the end of the lane there was the village, and at the crossroads in the village there was a signpost that read LONDON.

I was going to follow the direction of that sign and keep going till I got there.

I was going home.

A week ago I'd no idea I'd be running away from Pinnock's Farm. Two weeks ago I'd never even heard of the place.

All this was a very long time ago, at the beginning of the war.

The war. Hitler's War. World War Two.

To start with, things didn't seem too bad.

When the war started everyone expected death and destruction to start raining down out of the sky. We'd all seen it in a film by H. G. Wells, called 'The Shape of Things to Come'. Whole cities destroyed by terrible bombing raids. The funny thing was, it didn't happen, not at first anyway. To begin with nothing much happened, as if neither side was quite sure what they ought to do next.

My dad dug an Anderson shelter in our back garden. Mum and I helped, digging as much as we could and carrying away loose earth in a bucket, but Dad did most of the work. He was small but tough, my dad, and he could turn his hand to anything. We had the finest Anderson for miles around.

First of all he dug a big square hole, like an underground room. He roofed with curved corrugated sheets of metal, provided by the Government. He put on a back bit, a front bit with a door, and then covered the lot with the earth he got from digging the hole. That was just the outside. Inside you needed boards for the floor and bunk beds to sleep on and a primus stove to make cups of tea and a paraffin lamp for light – all sorts of things to make it a second home.

The Anderson was ready months before it was used. The nights were peaceful and the war was something happening far away, and my dad got teased by his mates down the pub.

Then the bombers came.

I'd go to bed in a state of wild excitement and just lie there waiting. Usually, for all my determination, I'd just drop off, and Mum would wake me up, saying it was time for school. But other nights, more and more nights as time went on, I'd wake to the long howl of the air raid siren and Dad would lift me out of bed and carry me, wrapped in a blanket down to my second bed in the shelter.

I'd feel the coolness of the night air on my face and catch a glimpse of the long fingers of the searchlight beams wavering across the sky and the plump silvery shapes of the barrage balloons and see the flashes of the anti-aircraft guns.

Then I'd be tucked up again in the gloom of the shelter with the shadowy shapes of my mum and dad moving about and talking in low voices. There'd be cocoa made in advance in a thermos flask and a biscuit from the special tin.

Next morning I'd wake up, sometimes still in the shelter, sometimes back in my proper bed, and get up to go to school.

Even that was an adventure. I'd meet my mates in the street and we'd check to see how much of our familiar surroundings were still there. There was always some bomb damage to be seen but it always amazed me how little. It seemed as if London was so old and so massive it was going to take a heck of a long time to knock it all down.

One building that was always untouched was our school.

My best mate Eddie said it was because the headmaster had made a secret pact with Hitler – he was going to be Dictator of England if Hitler won. Another friend, Johnny, wanted to light a beacon on the school roof to guide the bomber in, but we convinced him it would be unpatriotic.

Most mornings we'd make ourselves late for school by hunting for shrapnel, chunks of jagged metal fragments, all that was left of the exploded bombs. Stamp collecting was nowhere that year.

I thought it was all wonderful. But my mum and dad didn't and now I can see why.

One morning I woke up to find a gaping, smoking hole where the end house in the street used to be. A nice family called the Strettons, cheerful dad, pleasant mum and two little girls. They'd just moved into the house and done it up and they were pleased as anything with it. Now there was no more house and no more Strettons.

Next morning my mum woke me up extra early.

'Wossamarrer?' I groaned. 'Stoo early for school.'

'You're not going to school,' said Mum briskly. 'You're going for a little holiday.'

I was all for it, and I jumped eagerly out of bed and started to get dressed. I didn't know that the holiday was Pinnock's Farm, or that it was a holiday for one.

We had a long, slow, crowded train journey. An even longer and slower bus journey and a long walk down a country lane to get to Pinnock's Farm. And when we got there I wasn't sure it was worth it. It wasn't much of a place, just a low stone farmhouse surrounded by a muddy yard with a huddle of scruffy outhouses.

To me it looked like a dump in the middle of nowhere.

Standing in the yard staring at us was a big, shock-headed loutish-looking boy. He was the Pinnocks' son and his name was Patrick. I was to get to know him better, or rather worse, before very long.

A big shapeless woman in a flowered apron came out of the house and stared at us as if we were invading Martians.

'Don't you remember me, Norah?' said Mum with a strained smile. 'Cousin Nelly from London.'

They went inside the farmhouse. I bent to stroke the black-and-white dog stretched out by the door.

'You leave him be,' ordered Patrick. 'He bites.'

Ignoring him, I held out the back of my hand for the dog to sniff, moving slowly, the way Dad had taught me with strange dogs. The dog sniffed my hand then licked it, and I ruffled his shaggy head. His tail thumped the ground. Patrick moved closer, amazed. The dog bared its teeth in a snarl.

After what seemed a long time, Mum hurried out of the farmhouse. She gave me a hug and pressed half-a-crown in my hand. 'Just you be good now – I'll come and see you as much as I can.'

Suddenly I realised the awful truth. I was being abandoned, alone, at Pinnock's Farm.

Before I could protest, Mum vanished into the gathering dusk. Mrs Pinnock took me into the kitchen for a huge supper. I couldn't eat.

In the week that followed I went around like someone shell-shocked, unable to take in what had happened to me. I felt I'd lost everything all at once: my house; my parents; my mates; Grandma and Grandad and all the uncles and aunts who lived nearby . . .

I even missed school.

The Pinnocks were decent enough. But they never said much, and when they did it was about farming, or about people I didn't know. There were no rows of shops, no cinemas, they didn't even have a radio. No electricity either, come to that. They used oil lamps. It was like going back in time.

I was missing London desperately, bombs and all.

I suppose I might have got used to things in time – if it hadn't been for Patrick. A big, bony brute, much older than I was, Patrick hated me on sight. He was a bully and a slob. He whacked the cows as hard as he could with his stick when he drove them to be milked.

He tormented all the animals in his charge. Most of all he tormented me.

He was still at it at the end of that first week. In the kitchen, after supper, he jabbed me painfully in the ribs with one bony finger. 'Cry baby, cry baby, wants his mama, wants his mama . . .'

Blind with rage I took a flying leap at him, bowling him over by the sheer fury of my attack. For a minute or two we scrabbled about on the kitchen floor, till Mrs Pinnock heaved us apart. 'Just you stop that playing about in my kitchen. Patrick, you go and help your dad.' She turned to me. 'As for you my lad, you best go up to bed if you can't behave.'

As we separated and scrambled to our feet Patrick muttered, 'I'll get you for that tomorrow – cry baby!' He gave me a final vicious jab in the ribs and slouched off to the farmyard. As I climbed the stairs to my attic I already knew what I was going to do . . .

It was a mad scheme of course, and if I'd had a bit more sense I'd never have tried it. I'd no real idea of how far away London was, or even where it was. Luckily for me it was a mild, moonlit night, and I hurried along the road to the village, carried along by the excitement of the adventure. The cottages, shop and pub were all dark and silent, and soon I was at the crossroads beyond the village, staring up at the sign. LONDON 50 MILES. (Most of the road signs had been taken down to confuse the enemy, but they hadn't got to this one yet – either that, or they thought even Hitler would never bother to invade Pinnock's Farm.)

I walked and walked and walked, and gradually excitement gave way to exhaustion. I'd no real idea what a mile was of course, let alone fifty. Then I turned the corner and saw the lorry. It was an army lorry, a huge thing with a canvas hood, and beside it crouched two weary, sweating figures. They were just finishing changing a wheel, and I watched as they tightened the nuts. One of them straightened up. 'Think she'll get us there?'

'Search me,' said the other soldier gloomily.

'Maybe we'd better turn back to the depot.'

'What, and face the sarge? Vital supplies to go to the docks, that's what he said. So, that's where we go. Didn't they tell you there's a war on?'

They climbed into the cab. Soon I heard the roar of the engine. By that time I was already scrambling over the tail-board of the lorry.

The docks were very close to where we lived.

The lorry was crammed with big wooden packing cases, but I managed to find a space and curled up like a cat in the darkness.

The lorry rumbled on, and somehow in spite of the hard floor and the jolting I drifted into sleep, and a confused dream about going to the seaside in a tank.

I woke up very suddenly when a sharp jolt threw me against the nearest packing case. The lorry had stopped.

I crawled to the back and lifted the canvas.

All around the world seemed to be in flames. London was burning, just like the old nursery rhyme.

I climbed out of the lorry and found myself in what little was left of a London street, most of its buildings reduced to blazing rubble. There was a fire engine at the far end trying to save a blazing house, and I could see men from the heavy rescue squad digging in the ruins of another. Looming over the street was the huge round shape of a gasometer, sending up a fountain of fire that made the scene all round as bright as day.

An air-raid warden was talking to the soldier at the wheel of the lorry.

'You'll have to turn back, mate, the roads ahead are blocked. The gasworks here's just copped it, and the docks as well. Worst raid of the war, they reckon.'

I was too excited to be afraid. I'd suddenly realised exactly where I was. The gasworks were even nearer to us than the docks. I was only a few streets away from home. I looked at the desolation all around me. If home was still there, I thought, and turned and ran.

The Warden caught sight of me as I left the shelter of the army lorry. 'Oi, you!' he yelled. 'Get yourself in a shelter. The nearest's in Market Street.'

'On my way,' I shouted, and sprinted round the corner. But the shelter I was making for was the one in our back garden.

From behind me came the distant whistle and crash of exploding bombs, but the amount of bomb damage seemed less as I got nearer home. We'd been caught by the edge of a raid meant for the docks.

When I got into our street there was no fresh damage at all, just the rubble-strewn hole that had once been the Strettons' house.

Our house was dark and silent as I opened the side gate that led into the back garden.

There was a shallow hole with a rim of earth round it beside the Anderson as if Dad had decided to build a second shelter. I went to the shelter entrance and pulled aside the blackout curtain. 'Mum? Dad?'

No one answered.

The lamp was still lit and there were two cups of still-warm cocoa poured from the thermos. But the shelter was empty.

I stared round unbelievingly for a moment then ran

out of the shelter. I crossed the garden, jumping the new hole, and went back into the street. A tin-hatted figure grabbed me by the arm. For a moment I thought it was the first of Hitler's invading hordes but it was only Mr Morrissey, our local air-raid warden, a bad-tempered old codger with round glasses and a droopy moustache.

We gazed at each other in mutual astonishment. 'What are you doing here?' he wheezed. 'Heard you was in the country.'

'I was, but I came back,' I said impatiently. 'Where are my mum and dad?'

'Evacuated.' Mr Morrissey pronounced the word with professional relish.

'Evacuated? What to the country, like me?'

It was a bit thick, I thought, if I'd come all the way back here only to find my family carted off to somewhere like Pinnock's Farm.

'No just evacuated out of the shelter. Whole street's been evacuated. I was just checking everyone was gone.'

'Why? What for?'

'Unexploded bomb.'

'Where?'

'Where?' repeated Mr Morrissey in outraged tones. 'Only in your blessed back garden, that's where. Didn't you see the hole?'

I swallowed hard. 'Yes, I suppose I did. Look, please, where are they?'

Mr Morrissey sucked his teeth. 'Where? Depends where they took 'em. Could be anywhere by now.' He looked down at my stricken face and added grudgingly, 'You could try the Tube . . .'

Almost before he'd finished speaking I was off and running down the street. People who didn't have a shelter of their own, or didn't feel safe in one, were

allowed to sleep on the platforms on the underground.
I ran to the other end of our street then turned into the
High Street. It was empty, eerily lit by the flames from
the burning docks and gasworks.

At the entrance to the underground I bumped into
another warden. 'Full up,' he said, jokingly.

'Please,' I gasped, 'I think my mum and dad are down
there. We got separated.'

'Off you go then, sonny. Always room for a little 'un.
Lifts aren't working, you'll have to use the stairs . . . '

I ran down what seemed to be an endless spiral staircase
and emerged panting on to the platform which was filled
with a long row of blanket-bundled sleeping forms.
People were just getting settled down to sleep but I
soon put a stop to that.

'Mum, Dad!' I roared. 'Where are you? I'm back!'

There was an answering shout from the other end of
the platform and I hurdled the indignant stretched-out
forms like a steeplechaser until I collided full tilt with a
figure coming the other way.

Dad gripped my shoulders and stared down at me
amazed. 'You're supposed to be out in the country.'

'Didn't like it, Dad, so I came back.'

Dad gave me the look that said he didn't know
whether to hug me or clip my ear. To my relief, he
settled for the hug. 'Well, now you're back, I suppose
you'll have to stay. Come and say hullo to your mum.'

The unexploded bomb never did explode. The bomb
squad fixed it and carted it away, refusing to let me keep
it for a souvenir.

Nobody tried to make me go back to Pinnock's Farm.

Mum wrote to her cousin apologising for my sudden departure.

We stuck it out through the blitz till Dad got called up in the army. He finished up Quartermaster-Sergeant in an army camp in the North, and after a time Mum and I moved up to join him.

It was a few years before we saw London again, but we stayed together.

Hitler never did manage to burn London down. After the war we came back home again, and had victory parties in the street.

I swore I'd never move away again – and I never did.

Berlie Doherty

I was born in Liverpool and spent most of my childhood in a small seaside town called Hoylake, which I loved. I now live in another city, Sheffield, which is surrounded by some of the most beautiful countryside in England. When I first moved here we lived right on the outskirts of the city in a house that overlooked a valley full of fields and trees, with two reservoirs in the distance. I could go for long walks just by stepping over the peat wall at the bottom of my garden. There's a housing estate now where the fields began, and the cottages at the bottom of the hill have all been demolished. I was with my three children in the donkey field which is now a new housing estate when I first saw the daylight owl. I'll never forget how excited we all were to see him, and how sad we felt when we knew that his hunting ground had gone for ever.

Now I live on the other side of the city. I drive out into the countryside to go for walks. That's where I think up my stories. I'm a city dweller, but I hate a day to pass without seeing something of hills and valleys and rivers, and the wild life that has its home there.

White Peak Farm was serialised in 1988 on BBC1. In 1987 the Carnegie medal was awarded to Granny Was a Buffer Girl. Owls are Night Birds has been broadcast on BBC Radio 4 Morning Story.

Owls Are Night Birds

Elaine was always a little in front of Steven as they scrambled up the slope. It was so steep that they had to heave themselves up by clinging on to the coarse sprouting grass. When Elaine hauled herself up at last on to the top path she stood watching Steven, not helping him, as loose stones scuttled under his feet.

'Hot!' she gasped. 'Too hot!'

The path was dusty and rutted. It would lead them through the donkey field, past the new housing estate and the infant school, and on up the hill to their home.

'Come on, Steven.' Elaine set off again as soon as her brother had pulled himself over the tip of the slope. For a moment he lay on the grass at the side of the path, listening to the thud of her feet. Far away he could hear the drone of the city, like a hushed roar. The sound never stopped, day and night. It was the sound of foundries, hammering like a heart. It was the sound of cars and lorries and buses, always on the move, like blood pumping through veins. It was the sound of half a million people breathing.

He felt as if he was drowning in the stale air of the city's breath. 'I'm a lizard,' he thought. 'I'll dry up here in the sun; then she'll be sorry.' He stood up and ran along after her, stooping to search through the dense foliage for bilberries. He found some that the birds had left, and crouched down so he could cram them into his mouth. 'They're saving my life,' he thought. 'She'll die.'

'I'm sick of you,' his sister shouted, impatient. 'Come on. I'll buy you some lemonade at Mr Dyson's, if you hurry.'

'Race you to the donkey field!' he yelled, and she took up his challenge and broke into a loose run as the path flattened and swung into the shelter of overhanging trees. He stumbled after her, his shoes slapping the hard earth, watching the swing of her yellow hair. 'Can't make it. I'm a dead man.' He nursed a stitch that bent him sideways. He watched Elaine as she clambered up the leaning stone wall that surrounded the donkey field. She held herself there, motionless, with her hand lifted to shield her eyes. He limped up to her, drawing in his breath and groaning so that she wouldn't laugh at him for losing the race, but she swung her arm behind her in a warning gesture, and he pulled himself up beside her and sat with his legs straddling the hump of the wall; silent.

He saw immediately what she was looking at. A large white bird moved across the field towards them; a bird with a broad heavy head and wide blunt wings. It swung upwards, its great wings driving it like a swimmer through still water, and it drifted, bullet-headed, a huge silent moth, lifting itself soundlessly, while the air hung quiet around it. In the middle of the field the donkeys pressed and nudged each other, flicking their ears idly, unconscious of the dark shadow gliding over them.

'What is it?'

'It's an owl,' said Elaine softly. She couldn't take her eyes off it.

Steven slid off the wall and lay with the long grass criss-crossed over him. 'But owls are night birds.' He followed the slow flight of the bird quartering the field. With a last wide sweep that swung it high above their heads it left the field and floated across the wide valley, and was lost among the dark trees that shadowed the river on the far side; miles away.

Elaine slid down beside him and they trudged across the field. Steven pointed out some deep trenches that had been cut across the far end. They stretched out in a line from the end of the housing estate to the village lane, and they seemed to be huge squares dug into the soil. They walked slowly round them.

'What d'you think these are?' Steven asked. 'Why should someone dig up the donkey field?'

'I dunno,' said Elaine. 'Donkeys had better watch it, or they'll drop in.'

They both giggled.

'Come on,' said Steven. 'Let's ask Mr Dyson about that bird.'

He raced away from her, and she followed him slowly, her mind on the great white bird with sunlight like cream across its back.

Mr Dyson's corner shop was at the end of the lane that led up to their house. From there he'd sold sweets and drinks to generations of children on their way to and from school. You could hardly call it a shop now. At one time it had been crammed with ropes and buckets and bacon and socks and all the oddments that people in a village might want to buy in a hurry. But then, a few years ago, old Mr Dyson had had a stroke, and the village people had started going down to the supermarket that had opened up on the main road down to the city. Mr Dyson's stroke had left him partially paralysed. He never went out any more. His wife had kept the shop going so that at least he'd see the people who came in to buy, and they were mostly children, who knew that they could spend all the time in the world making their choices. She baked daily, and the warm sweet smell of new-baked bread and cakes snapped at you as you came up the hill, drawing you in. The shop part was really their front room, and at the jingle of the bell, old Mr Dyson would struggle out of the back room and greet the visitor with a shout of pleasure.

'I'll give you some money,' Elaine said. 'I'll wait out here.' Steven pulled her in. She was frightened of Mr Dyson now. His body was curiously twisted, so that one arm hung useless and one leg dragged to the side, and he walked with a laborious hopping rock-shuffle. His speech slurred one consonant into the other, making it impossible for anyone to understand him without watching his eyes, and Elaine was frightened of doing this. Usually she pushed her money across the counter to him and took her sweets and ran, letting the door jangle shut behind her and breathing in the outside air. But Steven loved him. He would climb on to the high stool that was put out for people who couldn't choose their sweets in a hurry and he and Mr Dyson would struggle to talk to each other. Sometimes, if they got stuck, Mrs Dyson would come out from the back and translate for them. She was sad and old and little, and hardly ever smiled.

Today Mr Dyson was dispirited. He leaned across the counter with his good arm, flapping his hand at the wasps that buzzed above the sticky cakes.

'Hey! Mr Dyson!' Steven shouted as he ran in.

The old man looked up, pleased. 'Hey! Hey!' he shouted back, and nodded to the cane stool. 'What have you two been up to today?' he seemed to say. You could just tell by the vowels.

'Mr Dyson! Wait till I tell you what we've seen!'

Elaine hung back. After the brilliance of the summer sunshine the shop was dark and gloomy. It was as if all that daylight no longer existed. She hated the dim stuffiness of the place. She watched the strip of yellow sticky paper that hung from the light bulb above the counter. It was stuck with the dead and dying bodies of wasps and flies and bluebottles, and it swivelled round slowly with the draught of air they'd brought in with them from outside. She longed to dive back out into the sunlight again.

'It was a bird, Mr Dyson, a great white one, like a ghost.'

'Like an owl,' said Elaine, cross.

'But it couldn't have been an owl, could it? They're night birds.'

Elaine wanted to tell him about the strange coldness it had put on them. Maybe that was what Steven had meant.

Mr Dyson frowned and nodded and called his wife in to help him out, and she came in with a jug of home-made lemonade that was all frothy and cloudy and swimming with pips, and poured some out for the two children.

'Come on Elaine,' she said, and Elaine edged forward and sat awkwardly on the other chair. The woman watched her husband as he talked, and spoke to him in the same sort of brief unfinished words. He seemed very tired, and kept shifting his position. The children drank, watching them.

'He reckons it's a barn owl,' Mrs Dyson said at last. 'An albino barn owl. A bit of a freak. That's why it's so white. And if its hearing and eyesight are weak, then it can't hunt by night, so it has to come out by day when seeing's easier. Fancy, he says, by all them new houses.'

Mr Dyson muttered something again and she translated it, but Steven beat her to it with a laugh of triumph.

'He says we're a pair of lucky jiggers to see it, an' all.'

Mr Dyson shook his head and swung his heavy body round, as if he were tired of this conversation, and heaved himself into the back room. His wife took the glasses from the children and put them on her tray.

'When he was a young man,' she told them quietly, 'he liked nothing better than to be up walking in the hills. You could walk for miles in them days, either direction, and still be in the country. And birds was his hobby, watching birds all hours, when he was young, and well.'

'We saw something else as well,' Steven said. 'Big holes. In the field.'

Mrs Dyson shook her head at him and looked quickly towards the back room, as if making sure that her husband hadn't heard. Then she took the tray into the back without saying goodbye, and Steven and Elaine left their money on the counter and went outside, squeezing past the door so they didn't make the shop bell jangle.

A few days later Elaine and Steven went back to the donkey field, and there was the barn owl again.

'Barney!' Steven whispered, watching it.

They both felt the same thrill of excitement and strange surge of uneasiness as the air became silent and the bird moved strongly and soundlessly round them, and at last drifted away to its home.

'Tell him! I'm going to tell him!' Steven shouted. His heart was thudding with excitement as he raced out of the field to Mr Dyson's shop. Elaine trailed after him, and stopped to look at the holes in the earth. They were deeper now. They were proper trenches, roped off in big squares. A huge yellow fork-lift truck was parked by the gate, and beyond it, a workmen's portacabin. She walked down past the end hole square. After that was the new road, and beyond that, the housing estate. She could see nothing but houses from there, spreading down the long hill in a pattern of pink and grey roofs, down, down, to the far throbbing valley that was the heart of the city.

'Hey!' Mr Dyson laughed as Steven burst into the shop.

'Hey!' said Steven. 'We've seen it again!'

Mr Dyson chuckled as he listened to Steven, indicating that he wanted him to crawl under the counter flap and to come through with him to the back of the cottage. Mrs Dyson was baking. The room was neat and small, and as dark as the shop. Mr Dyson knelt down on one knee with his bad leg stretched behind him and searched through a pile of oddments under the table. At last he fished out what he was looking for. It was a large book.

'*Bird Journal*,' Steven read. 'Is this from when you were young and well, Mr Dyson?'

Mrs Dyson swung round to chastise him, but the old man chuckled and fingered through the carefully hand-written pages with their listings and sketches of birds he'd observed. He folded the book back on its first clean page.

'Pen, love,' he sounded to his wife, and she, floury and smiling now, found him one.

'Barn owl', he wrote.

'Barney,' Steven told him, and Mr Dyson wrote it in

brackets next to the heading. 'Sighted, 3 p.m. Friday, August 3rd and Tuesday, August 7th. The donkey field.'

Mrs Dyson found some pencils and Steven sketched the owl in flight, and when he left Mr Dyson was sitting at the kitchen table, his tongue pressed out between his teeth like a child's, shading in Steven's sketch with coloured pencils.

Elaine was waiting for Steven outside the shop. 'They're building,' she told him.

'Building?' he repeated, puzzled.

'In the donkey field. They're building something there.'

'They can't,' he said flatly. 'It's the last bit of country left before the city. They can't build there.'

'Anyway,' he thought. 'It belongs to Barney now, that field.'

From then on the donkey field was Steven's favourite haunt. Elaine went with him a couple of times but by the time she'd seen Barney twice more she was bored. At least, that's what she told Steven. She loved to watch the owl's slow flight, but she hated the drone of the trucks and building lorries down at the bottom of the field, and the loud shouts of the workmen. She hated what she was seeing, as the earth holes were filled in with cement and tons of red bricks were tipped out nearby.

And she dreaded the visits to Mr Dyson's afterwards. The dimness and the stuffiness of the shop closed round her like winter nights, chasing away the summer. She felt strangely as if the donkey field and Barney were things they'd made up for the old man's benefit. For the first time ever, Steven and Elaine started to drift apart. They didn't even realise it was happening.

'Coming to the donkey field?' Steven asked her one

day. She shrugged and followed him slowly out of the house, and then just didn't bother to go down the road after him, and he didn't bother to go back for her. She watched him running off down the hill, and couldn't explain the sadness she felt inside herself. She rang up a school friend and arranged to meet her in town, and they spent that day and most of the rest of the holiday touring the boutiques and trying on new clothes. She wanted to look like the city girls, who always looked fresh and bright. She was sick of the country clothes she wore at home, all faded cottons and old jeans. They made her look too young.

'Guess what my brother's doing now?' she said to her friend, Anna, one day. 'He's lying in a donkey field.'

'What for?' Anna asked, astonished.

'Watching a silly old owl!'

The two girls exploded into giggles, and turned themselves round in front of the shop mirror, admiring themselves in the dresses they couldn't afford to buy.

Mr Dyson loved Steven's visits. He wrote up his journal every day. Once Steven found an owl pellet near the trees and carried it, warm in his hand to the old man; a trophy, to the dark room where Mr Dyson had imprisoned himself. They rolled it open and sketched the tiny mouse bones they found in it. Mr Dyson had long forgotten the misery and resentment he'd felt when he first heard about Barney. The pellet was his find now, just as much as it was Steven's.

Sometimes Mrs Dyson would stand at the doorway of the shop watching out for Steven. 'Come on, love! He's waiting!' she'd sing out, and she'd leave the shop door propped open to let in the daylight. She brought flowers into the house and bustled round them while they talked, or sat, listening peacefully to their strange and awkward conversations. For the first time in years she forgot to be worried about her husband. She coaxed him into their little back garden where he could sit out and watch the cloud patterns on the far hills, and read the bird books Steven brought him from the library. And whenever Steven came there was always a glass of golden ginger beer or pale lemonade or apple juice for him, and new scones spread with home-made jam with strawberries whole and plump in it.

Sometimes they heard trucks trundling past on their way to the field. They seemed to make the whole cottage shake. Mr Dyson would look at his wife, worried and questioning, and she would look at Steven, willing him to keep his mouth shut. Steven always stopped to look at the buildings as he came past. The squares of bricks were as high as his waist now, and there was a gap in the front and the back of every one of them, just wide enough for someone to go in and out.

And then Barney left the field. Day after day Steven ran down there and lay in the long grass scanning the sky. He would race down on his way to the big shops on the estate, or first thing in the morning, or early evening, and the donkeys would always trot over and nuzzle him. But he hadn't come for the donkeys, or for the looping swallows. He was convinced that the albino owl had died. One day the donkeys were gone from the field too, and another row of trenches had been dug. He ran down to the first lot of buildings. The lines of bricks were higher. Rectangular spaces were left on all the sides. The holes that were big enough to walk in and out of were covered over at the top, and he knew for the first time what he had known in his heart for weeks. 'Doors!' he said out loud. 'Houses! They've joined us up with the city.'

He picked up a handful of rubble and started chucking it through the doorways and window holes, enjoying the thud of it as it spattered against the inside walls.

'Oi!' One of the builders yelled at him. 'What you up to? Eh?'

'You've killed Barney!' Steven shouted. 'This is his hunting field. You've killed him!'

The man shouted at him to clear off, and Steven ran home, straight past Mr Dyson's shop, not even looking. For the next few days he kept going down to the field, just in case, and he came slowly past the shop. Sometimes he just tapped on the window and shook his head.

He spent all Saturday in the field when the workmen were not working. He wandered miserably round the buildings, wondering if he could get the cement mixer to work, thinking about filling in all the door and window holes, and he knew that it was useless. The city had come, and there was no stopping it. He heard a great roar surge up from somewhere far below, and he ran to the edge of the field, listening. It was the sound of a football match. It was a goal. He heard the excited chanting of the crowd and found his own voice in it, 'Ci-ty! Ci-ty! Ci-ty!' he murmured, and then louder and louder, yelling it out, a thrill of excitement inside him. 'CI-TY!'

And that was the last day of the summer holidays. He and Elaine started back at school the next week. They never sat together on the bus any more. She had her own friends now.

Mr Dyson sat all day at his table, waiting for the boy to come. He listened inside himself for Steven's animated chatter that had brought so much of the summer sunshine into his dark home. His house had grown gloomy and quiet again. He was lost for things to do, and Mrs Dyson became anxious and unsmiling again, watching him. He kept his journal open and ready on the table, and at the end of the day he would write with his good hand, 'No Barney today.'

'No Steven today,' Mrs Dyson would say, looking over his shoulder. That was what he meant.

When the letter came from the council telling them that the cottages in their lane were to be demolished to make way for the new development she hid it in fear from him. She spent hours in her garden, pulling up weeds uselessly. 'It's coming, it's coming,' she said to herself. 'There's no stopping cities.' They'd have a modern house with proper facilities. They'd be surrounded. It would make a change. It would break the old man's heart.

The last day in September was brilliantly sunny. Steven and Elaine had nothing to do, and decided to go down to the river together. Steven was shy about asking Elaine to come with him now. They picnicked there and she lay back, catching a last suntan, while Steven skimmed pebbles on the water and watched the wagtails and dippers bobbing on the stony banks. They'd come the long way because that would bring them back on their favourite walk past the farm with the goats and eventually, up the long hill to the donkey field. They didn't mention Barney to each other. He belonged to a part of the summer that was past.

'Race you to the donkey field!' he challenged as they panted up the slope.

'Not a donkey field now!' she reminded him. 'Housing estate.'

They scrambled up the last steep slope and Elaine swung along the path, with Steven close behind her, and as they clambered up the stone wall there it was again;

the white owl, in the full brilliance of the late afternoon: Barney. Low over the grass, and below them, with its broad strong head and its pale soft back, quartering the field of half-grown houses with slow lifts of its wings. There was no other movement in the field. Not a sound.

Elaine and Steven stood, breathless, on the wall, following Barney's route across the field, and suddenly Steven's eyes were stopped by an unfamiliar bundle in the grass, a twist of drab colour, humped at an angle. He turned sharply to Elaine and she smiled and nodded and laid her hand on his arm. Mr Dyson, lying in the long grass at the side of the field, raised his arm slowly as if in a salute, and rested his hand as a shield above his eyes, watching the movements of the daylight owl.

Steven thought of the old man dragging himself to the front of his shop; his slow unsteady shuffle. It must have taken him hours to get himself down the lane, past the little school, through all the rubble of the building site and across the rough grass to where he lay now, folded in a corner of the field. He forgot to watch Barney, and when he looked again the bird was making its last circle of the field. It rose higher and higher, right into the line of the sun, nearly blinding him, and then it drifted out across the valley to its dark shelter. Steven knew that he would never see it again.

The voice of the city surged up like a throaty roar and died away again. Steven plunged across the grass to the old man.

'What d'you think of Barney, Mr Dyson? I told you, didn't I?'

Mr Dyson lay with his hand still resting across his eyes, like a small child suddenly fallen asleep. The boy stood back a little, and his sister joined him. Together they looked down at the old man, with the grass criss-crossed against his face, and the small bees droning round him, and the sun warm on him.

Elaine put her arm round Steven's shoulder.

'We'd better go,' she told him. 'We'd better tell her.'

'But, he isn't asleep, is he?' said Steven doubtfully, staring down at the old man, at the humped twist of his body and the strange expression of peace on his face.

'No. He isn't asleep. He's all right.'

And the brother and sister walked slowly from their summer field in silence together.

Anne Fine

I wrote my first book, The Summer House Loon *marooned in a high flat in Edinburgh with a baby during a fierce winter when the streets were so icy it was impossible to push the pram up the hill to the central library or down the hill to the nearest branch library. I'd read every book in the house. It was a matter of reading the back of the cornflake packets or writing my own. That was sixteen years ago. I've now published over a dozen books, mostly for children.*

Although I spent several years away in America and Canada, I'm now back in the same flat. I have two teenage daughters, a golden retriever, two cats and two goldfish. As the years go by, I seem to spend less and less time with the children, and more and more with the dog. We spend hours walking through city parks and streets – and to the libraries!

I've had a series of jobs. I worked for Oxfam, taught in a prison and a girls' school, and worked in an art gallery. But I always come back to writing, though it's not my greatest pleasure. I much prefer reading: newspapers; magazines; poetry; novels. When I was at school, careers advice was simple: decide what you like doing most in the world, then look for the job that pays you to do it. I'm halfway there.

My only other claim to fame is that, because I have four sisters myself (all married), and I married a man with five brothers, I happen to have nine brothers-in-law.

Fight the Good Fight

'I've heard of fighting the good fight,' the bus driver says to me almost every morning when I get off. 'But you are really weird.' He shakes his head. 'Really weird.'

He's quite wrong. I'm perfectly *normal*. There's nothing *wrong* with me. I'm probably about the same age as you. I'm probably about as clever, and I can take a joke, just like you. The only thing different about me is that I hate cigarette smoke. I just can't stand it. I think it stinks.

It's only the smell of it I hate. I quite like the way it looks. I used to love sitting on my mum's knee, watching the wispy streams of fine blue smoke float up from her fag ends (before I frightened her into giving up with all my talk of "coughin' nails"). I liked the way that, when she moved, or laughed, or waved her hand as she was talking, the smoke would twist and wind on its way up to the ceiling, and you could blow on it gently, till it drifted into great billowing circles.

And I liked watching my dad smoke his pipe, too (before he threw it in the rubbish after I saw a smoker's lungs on telly, all brown and kippery, and burst into tears). I liked the way he puffed out huge silvery-blue clouds, and smacked his lips, making little putt-putt-putt noises, whenever he thought it might be going out. He was an ace pipe-smoker, my dad – a real professional. He once kept it going all the way home from my granny's in a rainstorm.

Granny's the only one of my relations who smokes now (when she can stop coughing long enough to take a good puff). But since I only see her every other Saturday, I don't really mind.

What I mind is the bus.

My bus, the number 14, runs from one end of the city to the other. It's only a single decker, so in the mornings it gets terribly crowded, partly with people like me going to school, and partly with adults on their way to work. By the time the bus reaches my stop, Railton Dyke End, at ten past eight, there's hardly ever any seats left. I usually have to stand for fifteen minutes, till I get off at the end of Great Barr Street. And the bus is sometimes so crowded I get pushed further and further down the gangway.

And that's the problem. That's why the bus driver thinks I'm so weird. I can't stand moving further down the gangway. The front half of the bus is fine by me. It's all non-smoking, with little red stickers saying so on the windows, and nothing but clean bright-green peppermint wrappers stuffed in the ashtrays, and even a sign on the glass pane behind the driver's back that says *Have a heart – Stop smoking now*. But the back of the bus is disgusting. It's all grey-faced men and women wheezing and coughing and spluttering out clouds of their filthy-smelling grey smoke, and flicking their dirty ash flakes on one another's clothing, and leaving their fag ends smouldering in the overflowing ashtrays, and trampling their nasty little soggy yellow stubs on the floor in their hurry to get off the bus at the right stop, and light up another.

It's horrible. I hate it. I wouldn't mind so much if the

smell stayed down their end with them, and you could turn your back on the whole revolting spectacle and just pretend it wasn't there. But not only does stale smoke drift up to our end, but sometimes when the bus gets really crowded, the driver even tries to force you to move further along and stand at the filthy end, stop after stop, while the vile smell seeps into your clothes and your hair, and even your skin.

'Move along inside. Move down the bus *please*. You, too.' (He means me.)

'Did you hear what the driver said, little girl? Make room. Move along a bit.'

I cling desperately to the rail of the last pair of non-smoking seats.

'Sorry, I can't move down any further. That's the smoking end, and I don't smoke.'

Sometimes people glare. Sometimes they mutter. But, mostly, they just stare at me as if I were bonkers.

And I'm not. As I said at the start, I am a perfectly normal person. There's nothing weird about preferring half-way reasonable air to standing over some stranger's personal miniature chemical refinery, breathing in the waste fumes. I don't see why *I* should be forced to move down the bus.

'You clog up my gangway every morning,' the bus driver complains when I force my way up to the very front, to get off. 'You ought to be more co-operative.'

I don't see why. I wouldn't co-operate with putting my head in a noose. I wouldn't co-operate with throwing myself out of a helicopter without a parachute. I don't see why I should co-operate with getting my lungs black.

But when I tell him so as he slows down at the corner

of the street that leads to my school, he gets all snappy with me.

'You should go through the proper channels,' he tells me. 'You should stop making trouble on my bus.'

But I'd tried proper channels. Proper channels were perfectly useless, I can tell you. I got my mother to write a letter to the bus company, and all she got back was some very polite rubbish about 'fully appreciating her point of view', but 'having to consider the feelings of the other passengers'.

Well, what about *my* feelings? Don't they count? I catch the bus every single morning we have school. I have for years. That's over two hundred times a year. That's over a thousand bus rides *already*. I'd have to be a real drip not to fight back. So, over the years, I have developed my own private methods of making people stub their cigarettes out on the bus. (That's what the driver means by 'making trouble'.)

My first method is the best. It works the quickest, especially on motherly women with lots of shopping bags who are having their first quiet fag of the morning. Just as my victim lights up and leans back, sighing with pleasure, I lean towards her and, tugging a grubby old paper tissue out of my pocket, I start to snivel. If my victim doesn't notice, I sob a bit, quietly, and start my shoulders heaving up and down. I try to get real tears rolling down my cheeks, but that only tends to work if I get in the cigarette's slipstream.

After less than a minute the victim always asks kindly:

'Are you crying, little girl? What's the matter?'

'Nothing.'

I wipe my nose on the back of my hand, but sweetly, like a small child in a family film, not disgustingly, like Gareth Chatterton in primary four.

The victim leans forward and whispers:

'Come on, dear. You can tell me. Are you hurt?'

I shake my head.

'In trouble?'

'No-oo.'

'Is anyone at school picking on you?'

'No,' I say. 'It's not that. It's – ' I make my voice tremble. And then I hesitate, so she has to ask again.

'What is it, dear?'

Then I look her straight in the eye.

'It's my aunty,' I say. 'She used to smoke, too. The same brand as you. But now she's got – ' I pause, and watch the cigarette as it burns away between her fingers. Then, while the little word I'm *not* saying rings an alarm bell in my victim's brain, I finish up delicately:

'Well, she's very ill. She can hardly breathe now.'

At this point the victim always stubs out her fag, and looks thoughtfully at the little cardboard packet in her hand. I don't feel guilty. Why should I? Better she's my victim than the cigarette's, after all. And when it comes to getting a bit of fresh air on our bus, every quick stub-out helps.

I used this method a lot in the beginning. It worked a treat. The only problem was that the bus tends to carry the same passengers, day after day, so after a week or two only new passengers bothered to ask me why I was so unhappy.

So I moved on to Method Number two.

'I can smell fire!'

'Fire?'

'Fire!'

Everyone holds their fags up a little bit higher, and inspects them carefully. Then they inspect the folds in their clothing, and peer down between the bags and briefcases on the floor, to see if a burning cigarette has set something smouldering.

'Really. I can smell something burning. Can't you smell it? It's very strong.'

'It's just the cigarette smoke, dear.'

'Oh, no,' I argue. 'It couldn't just be cigarette smoke. It smells *disgusting*, and it's getting *worse*.'

One by one, people at the back are getting nervous and stubbing out their cigarettes just that little bit early.

'I can still smell it. I'm sure everyone can. There is a definite smell of burning. It's terribly strong, and very nasty.'

Sometimes I can get every single passenger at the back of the bus neatly stubbed out before we even reach the Safeways at the bottom of Dean Bank.

Then there's Method Number three. That's when I double over in a coughing fit, and make my face go pink, then red, then blue if it isn't Monday and I feel up to it. I cough and cough. I make a simply appalling noise. You'd think it was my lungs getting destroyed, not theirs. It sobers them up pretty quickly, I can tell you. Whole bus loads can't stub out fast enough when I get going.

Method Number four is a variation on number three. It's just a combination of coughing and glaring. I use it when there's only one smoker left who's pretending my coughing fit is nothing to do with their smoking.

Method Number five only works with women. I brush imaginary ash off my clothes. I brush and brush away, eyeing the cigarette, and soon the woman tries holding her fag in a different position. But I just keep on brushing. And in the end she begins to think that, wherever she holds it, her ash is going to float on to my clothing. Defeated, she stubs it out.

Now and then, miraculously, there's a free seat. If it's up the front, I take it. If it's at the back, I ignore it. I'd rather stand. But if it's in the last row between the smokers and the non-smokers, I take it and turn round to start conversations.

'Is that the brand with the coupons that get you the free iron lung?'

'Have you smoked for long?' (That always depresses them. They always have.)

If I've got a snack for my break-time, I start to unwrap it. Then I turn round and say:

'I hope my eating my granola bar isn't going to spoil your cigarette.'

Or I might kneel on the seat, lean over, and chat away merrily.

'We're doing a project on smoking at school. Did you know that there are over a thousand poisons in every cigarette? Did you know that one hundred thousand people every year die earlier than they should because they smoke? Did you know that if you live in the same house as smokers, you get to smoke eighty cigarettes a year without even having one? Did you know – ?'

Everyone at the back of the bus hates me. They all complain about me when they get off.

'That child's a real pain,' they say to the driver. 'She shouldn't be allowed to travel on this bus.'

He passes their sentiments on while I'm standing by his shoulder, waiting for my stop.

'They say you're a nuisance,' he tells me.

'Me?' I say, outraged. '*I'm* the nuisance? I like that!'

'There's not much to choose between you.'

'There most certainly is,' I argue. 'I'll tell you what there is to choose between us. If *they* stopped, *I'd* stop, straight away. If *I* stopped, they'd get *worse*. So I'd choose *me*.'

'None the less,' said the driver. 'I've had more than enough complaints. And until the company changes the rules, smokers are supposed to be welcome on this bus.' (You'll notice he didn't say they *were*. He only said they were *supposed* to be.) 'So, any more trouble from you, young lady, and I put you off at the next corner. Understand?'

Word travels faster than the number 14 bus. By the next morning, everyone knew that I was on probation. I only turned round once, and said quite amiably to the fellow behind me: 'Did you know smokers can get gangrene?' and the bus practically *screeched* to a halt. Before I knew what had happened I was standing on the pavement with my book bag and my gym shoes and my tennis racquet and my lunch box and my English folder and my choir music and a huge bag of dress-ups for the class play.

'I did warn you,' said the driver as the automatic doors went 'phut' in my face. 'Don't try to say I didn't warn you.'

I was twenty-five minutes late. Twenty-five minutes! I tried sneaking in the back way, but it was no use because, by the time I crept up the stairs to my classroom, Mrs Phillips had taken the register and marked me absent.

'Twenty-five minutes!' she scolded. 'Absolutely disgraceful. Be late again this week, and you'll be in big trouble.'

I really tried to keep quiet on the bus the next morning. It wasn't my fault I was forced so far down the gangway that I ended up standing over some fat old fellow who could scarcely *breathe*.

He spoke to me first – if you can call it speaking. It was more of a painful wheeze, really. He took his packet out of his pocket, opened it, peeped longingly at all the little killers inside, and closed it up again.

Then he glanced up and saw me watching him.

'Trying to give up,' he explained. 'Doctor's orders.'

Well I had to say *something*, didn't I? I was only being *polite*.

'You can do it!' I encouraged him. 'You can. You can! Fight the good fight! There are eleven million ex-smokers walking around Britain with good clean lungs. You can be the eleven millionth and first!'

That's *all I said*. And it wasn't him who got all shirty. It was the others who sent word up the gangway that I should be put off the bus again – all those not under doctor's orders. Yet.

'Enjoy the walk,' said the driver, pressing the button to shut the bus doors in my face. 'Phut'.

'Bye,' I said.

It wasn't so bad that morning. I only had my book bag and my lunch box and my recorder and my project on Witchcraft and my home-made peep-hole camera to carry. So I was only twenty minutes late.

'I did warn you,' said Mrs Phillips. 'That's a detention. You're twenty minutes late, so I want you in tomorrow twenty minutes early. You can write me an essay.' She fished about for a title that would do nicely for a punishment. 'I know. *A Business Letter*. And I want it properly set out and neatly written, with perfect spelling.'

I know when I'm beaten. I didn't argue. I just got up twenty minutes earlier the next morning, and caught the bus that comes twenty minutes earlier, and reached school twenty minutes earlier, and sat down to write.

Room 14
Stocklands School,
Great Barr Street,
21st April, 1988

Dear Sir or Madam,

I'm writing to tell you how bothered I am that some of the pupils in my class are forced to travel on buses each morning that are so thick with cigarette smoke that they arrive coughing, and with pink eyes. I have the number 14 bus particularly in mind.

In my view, smoking is for kippers, and children should be smokeless zones.

Please ban smoking on single decker buses as soon as possible, particularly the number 14.

Yours sincerely,

_____

I left the space at the bottom blank. I didn't sign Mrs Phillips' name in case she thought I was being cheeky.

How was I to know she'd sweep in and scoop it up, read it through, then sign her name with a flourish in the gap I'd left? How was I to know she'd root through the clutter in her desk to find an envelope, and send me off to the office to look up the bus company's address in the telephone directory? How was I to know she'd even dig in her own purse and give me a stamp?

She saw me looking at her.

'Fight the good fight,' she said.

The reply came a week later. I was surprised to see it was a bit different from the one my mother got back from them last year. There was a lot less of the 'considering the feelings of other passengers' stuff, and a lot more about 'coming to realise the hazards of passive smoking' and, 'frequent discussions on the possibility of changing bus company policy in this respect'.

'There you go,' said Mrs Phillips. 'They're half-way to cracking already. Just keep on at 'em.'

And so I do. I'm no trouble at all on the bus now. I've taken to getting up five minutes earlier so I can walk two stops back and catch the bus at the Ferry Lane Factory. (A lot of people get off there, so I get a seat.) I usually sit behind the driver. I look at his *Have a heart* no smoking sign for inspiration, then I dig out one of my four letter pads, and I write my letter.

I write one letter every single morning. (Mum buys the stamps. She says it's all in a good cause.) I write for everyone I know: family, friends, shopkeepers, penfriends, members of the gym club. Everyone signs their letter. Even Granny and the bus driver signed theirs. Granny says she wouldn't have gone to all the trouble of writing herself, being a smoker; but since I'd bothered it seemed a terrible waste not to post it. The bus driver said it's his bus and he's not allowed to smoke on it, so why should anyone else get away with it? It's not a very lofty attitude, I agree, but I didn't say anything. You see, I'm getting on a lot better with him now, since I started going through the proper channels.

He still thinks I'm weird. But he helps me with my

spelling if I get stuck, and he's even taken a couple of my letters home to get his wife and his sister to sign them.

And he lets me know whenever he hears rumours that all the single deckers are going non-smoking. It happens more and more often now. He thinks the change is coming. So do I. In fact, we're so sure that we've worked out which notice we're going to stick on the glass panel behind his seat on the Glorious Day. It's going to say, in big red capital letters:

WARNING
LIGHTING UP ON THIS BUS
CAN SERIOUSLY DAMAGE
YOUR HEALTH

I'll stop fighting the good fight then. But, if you see the number 14 going by, you'll still be able to recognize me. I'll be the one staring idly out of the window.

Michael Hardcastle

People who are aware of my books seem to think I'm obsessed with sport. I'm not. But I am exceedingly fond of it! Table tennis and snooker and garden cricket and outdoor bowls are what I play; soccer, motocross, any cricket, Rugby League, netball and horseracing are what I watch (with the Grand National as my favourite sporting event of the entire calendar). I started writing about sport as a novelist simply because I wanted to produce the sort of sports novel I would have enjoyed as a boy. In my childhood there weren't any sports books, only sports stories in comics and I wanted something longer than them. My 100th book, The Rival Games *(Methuen), published in May 1988, is, predictably enough, about a sports festival in a village that is honouring the memory of its most famous son, an Olympic hero of sixty years earlier. Yet the previous book,* Quake *(Faber), is all about an earthquake in England and the children who are trapped in a train and under a collapsed shopping centre. Most writers like to try something new and* Player Wanted, *my story in this collection, is the very first I've ever written in the first person, something I now know I'll want to try again. What isn't new is that it's about . . . football.*

Player Wanted

Last thing of all, Alastair went round shaking hands with everyone, something no one had ever done before. Then, without another word or a backward glance, he walked out of the changing-room. You could tell from the speed of his departure that he was full of emotion.

'We'll sure miss him,' observed Scott, stating the obvious as usual. 'We'll have to replace him. Otherwise we'll be finished. We might as well resign from the League now.'

'Look, he wasn't perfect,' Jason pointed out. 'Sometimes he missed chances other players would've netted with no trouble. And he didn't head many goals, did he? Wasn't all that great with his head. Didn't want to spoil his hair, did he, if the ball was a bit mucky? No, Alastair wasn't – '

'He was the best striker in the League, Jason, and you know it!' Scott retaliated. 'We'll never get another like him. I don't know how we're going to get *anybody* to join us. I mean, who wants to play for a team that's propping up the rest of the League? Nobody likes to get mixed up with a – a *flop*.'

'That's a bit of an exaggeration, Scott,' I put in mildly, half-agreeing with what he was saying but thinking that pessimism got you nowhere. 'I mean, we've won a few matches and Alastair wouldn't have left if his father hadn't decided to go and work in Spain. He reckoned we'd go places one day, even without his goals.'

'Yeah maybe, when you and me and Jason are dead and buried,' Scott muttered, reaching for his comb again and trying to add another suave swirl to the hairstyle he'd already spent ten minutes on. 'By then Partley United will be in the Heavenly League, too. Then they'll be able to call on all the talent they want!'

It wasn't all that bad a joke, for somebody like Scott, anyway, and Jason and I managed a laugh. Top soccer players are supposed to like gallows humour, or so we'd heard from Alastair's elder brother who'd had a few games for Rangers. At least in that sense, we were in good company. I thought Jason might say something about changing our name to change our luck. That was a regular subject for discussion because at times we became fed up with people (we couldn't call them supporters) joking about our suffering bad results because we were only partly united. Ha blooming ha! But Jason had been thinking of something quite different.

'We could advertise for a player, you know,' he said, almost nonchalantly.

'What!' Scott and I exclaimed in rare unison.

'Look, top clubs, well, *all* clubs, advertise when they need a new manager, don't they? So why shouldn't we put an ad in the paper for a new player?' Jason paused, but Scott and I were still too surprised to speak. So the skipper continued: 'There must be plenty of spare players hanging around looking for a team in this city. It's big enough. So we can let 'em know we have a vacancy, if they're interested.'

'Oh sure, I can just see them all queuing up to join us!' Scott scoffed. 'How does the ad go? "Bottom team needs brilliant striker. Must be guaranteed to score fifty goals a season. No pay and no prospects but loads of hard work." Oh sure, they'll come rushing, all right.'

'Depends how you word it,' Jason pointed out. He turned to me. 'That can be your job, Dave. You're the one who gets the best marks in English. So you can work out the best way to phrase the ad. OK?'

'Oh, er, yes, I suppose so,' I answered, too surprised by Jason's compliment to think of how to refuse. 'But where are we going to put this ad? In a newsagent's window or on that notice-board at the supermarket?'

'I said we'd advertise in a *newspaper*, didn't I?' Jason said in his most assertive mood. 'We've got to think big, in future. If things work out for us we might even get some free publicity from their sports department. Yeah, could be that – '

'But who's going to *pay* for the advert?' I interrupted before Jason escaped into another of his dreams. 'It won't be cheap in a paper like the *Herald*.'

His decision was almost instantaneous. 'We'll have a whip round among all the players. Everybody'll chip in something for a good cause like this. Look, I've got to get off now. See you at training on Tuesday night. You can bring the ad along then, Dave, and we'll go over it together. See you.'

'Best of luck,' Scott said as he departed. 'Reckon you'll need it to get anyone to reply to an ad for *our* team.'

'Oh, I don't know. Depends on how it's worded,' I replied, sticking to my new belief in optimism.

I rode home on my bike, thankful that at this time of day the roads weren't choked with the usual home-going traffic. Bike riding is supposed to help keep you fit but how can it when you have to weave a route through clouds of poisonous exhaust fumes?

That evening I must have spent an hour working on the advert. I knew that the cost depended on the number of words used, so every word had to count, in more senses than one. Could we afford a headline, something that would grab the attention of even the most casual reader of the *Herald*? Perhaps: 'Top Player Required', or: 'Make United Your Goal'. I really liked that one but eventually decided it was a bit vague. People might have imagined we were running a crusade of some kind whereas all we wanted was one player who could save us from disaster (on reflection, that *was* a crusade!).

No, it had to be clear and inviting. At about the tenth attempt I felt I'd got it right. Mr Bradbury, my English teacher, would have been proud of my industry as well as my determination to choose only the right words. 'Player wanted by keen youth team. Striker preferred. Phone 504030'. I knew that there might be objections, particularly about the use of the word 'preferred', but I'd argue that we really needed *anyone* who could play a bit. Perhaps there was a midfielder who was really good but fancied his chances of being a striker; if his own team wouldn't give him that opportunity then he could find it with us. Really talented strikers, like Alastair, were like gold and were not hanging around waiting for clubs to contact them. So we could hardly hope for the real thing.

I also worried about the adjective for us. After all, most teams are keen, aren't they, so why bother to mention it? Well, I thought the word lifted us out of the ordinary: it would appeal to a player looking for a team going places. I'd played with the idea of describing us as ambitious but then decided that might make us sound altogether too good, too showy. We definitely didn't want to deter a player who felt he might get into a reasonable team but would be out of place in a rising, successful outfit. As the Scotland manager is always saying about teams he chooses, 'I had to get the balance right.'

As it turned out, the rest of the United players were quite pleased with the advert, and only Scott had an objection. 'You should have given Jason's phone number, not your own, Dave. It's the captain's job to interview new players.'

'Dave's being a big help,' Jason replied. 'My dad usually keeps his answer machine on in the evenings because he doesn't want to be interrupted when he's watching the telly. But he hates it being cluttered up with calls for the rest of the family. So it might be tricky for players to get through to me.'

Scott still had to have the last word on that matter. 'Well, I just hope *somebody* wants to get through into our team. If they don't . . . '

After the ad was published I didn't quite sit at home by the phone, waiting for it to ring, but I stayed in earshot all that evening. It didn't ring once (which was also a blow to my sister who believed she'd just found a new boyfriend). I half expected a call from Jason to inquire how many candidates we had had, but perhaps he was having further problems with the family phone. The next day I carefully avoided Scott, who might have gloated about the advert being a duff idea. I took comfort from the thought that at least we hadn't put it in for two nights and therefore wasted even more money. As I walked home that afternoon after an uninspiring afternoon of oral French and awful science I pondered the possibility of finding another team for myself if United had to fold.

'You've had a mysterious phone call,' my mother greeted me. 'Won't give a name or a number or tell me what it's about. But he did mention an advertisement. Wants to meet you at seven by the pavilion in the park. David, what have you been up to?'

Of course, I had to give her some explanation and in the end she accepted that there was nothing sinister going on. After that the beefburgers and jacket potatoes tasted as good as they always did and I decided to walk to the park which lies beyond the cluster of tower blocks by the river and seems to sprawl all over what used to be dockland. I was elated: Jason's find-a-striker scheme had worked after all. I wished that Jason could have been with me but when I phoned his home all I got was that dumb answer machine (I mean, they leave *you* dumb, don't they?). Still, as a defender myself, I knew what we were looking for. If all went well, I might even be able to take our new team-mate round to Jason's home so he could meet our skipper.

There was just one boy, pacing up and down the wooden verandah, and I had no doubt he was waiting for me (not for one moment on the walk to the park had I feared that the mystery caller wouldn't turn up). His hair was short and blond and spiky, his build sturdy and strong; he wasn't tall but if he could jump that didn't matter. I'd met strikers like him before and knew how hard they were to dispossess once they were in sight of a goal. All muscle and hustle: and sometimes a bit savage if you got in their way at the wrong moment.

'You the one that put the ad in the paper?' he asked before I could say a word. He was looking over my shoulder as if surprised that I hadn't brought the rest of the team with me. I nodded and was about to ask his name when he rattled off a list of questions as if *he* was thinking of signing *me* up for a job. Once he knew the name of our team and the League we played in and that sort of thing his nervousness vanished and he stopped looking round every few seconds.

'Who do you play for?' I wanted to know. 'And are – '

'Don't play for anybody now,' he cut in. 'Used to, on the other side of the city – team you'll never have heard of. But then I – we – moved, moved house I mean. Scored a stack of goals for them. Played for City schoolboys, too – twice. Had a trial with Rangers, for a fact. Still, er, on their books. I'll get goals for your lot, no danger.'

I was impressed. He looked right and he sounded right. Strikers always have to have bags of confidence. I was sure I'd rather have this one on my side than play against me.

'Er, I don't know your name yet,' I pointed out.

'Ross. Ross Johnson. Look, can't hang around here any longer. Got a mate to see. But I'll be at your place for the game on Sunday. I'm never late. Got my own boots but bring me your strip, the number 9 shirt, OK? No other number.'

Then he moved off rapidly, hands thrust deep into the pockets of his black leather jacket and no backward glance. The meeting hadn't lasted as long as a half-time interval. But my instinct was that Ross Johnson would score the goals needed to lift Partley United up the League table.

* * *

Predictably, Scott could see problems ahead. 'How do we know he's going to turn up?' he asked several times as we changed before the game with Haxley, a team challenging for promotion. 'I mean, we're going to look damn stupid if we go out there without a real striker. We'll have to put one of the subs on and neither of them could score in a month of Sundays.'

'Just be thankful we've got subs,' Jason said mildly. 'Lots of teams are worse off than us, you know.'

'But we don't know anything about him, except what Dave's told us, and that's not much,' Scott, changing tack slightly, persisted. 'If we'd got his address we could have contacted him last night, this morning even, to give him a reminder about the match. You know, he could be taking the mickey out of us: just playing us up for laughs. Some idiots are like that.'

'Might even be a cunning plot by Haxley to make us think we'd got a new player when we haven't,' our goalie, Fergus, pointed out. 'Could be they set up that meeting with Dave.'

The ref had just popped his head round the door to tell us it was time to get on to the pitch when our new striker turned up, to everyone's relief (but mine more than anyone's, I suspect). He didn't volunteer any explanation as to why he was so late and because we were anxious to get him on to the pitch with us we didn't ask for one; Jason simply introduced everyone as quickly as possible and said he hoped Ross would bang in a hat trick. Ross just nodded as if he expected to do just that.

In our red-trimmed white shirt Ross looked even more powerful than I'd imagined and his strength was evident the moment he gained possession of the ball. Riding a couple of fairly awkward tackles, he hunched over the ball as though it would take a bulldozer to part him from it. Then, after hustling his way into the box he slid a pass inside the full-back for Scott to race on to and try a shot. Sadly, Scott's aim was woeful and the ball flashed high over the bar; but he stuck a thumb up at Ross to show he appreciated the precision of that pass. After that, Haxley decided they needed two men to mark Ross but even that didn't prevent him from scoring our first goal after ten minutes, a ferocious left-foot shot from twenty yards after he himself won the ball in a crunching tackle on one of his markers. Some of us blinked with astonishment at the quality of that strike.

Perhaps it was Ross's display that inspired Fergus, because he played a blinder: the finest game of his life, he admitted. Certainly he stopped everything Haxley threw at him apart from the flukiest of deflections that gave them their only goal. That score didn't matter because by then Ross had put the ball in the net again, this time from a penalty after he himself was fouled. His shot almost tore the net from its moorings. Haxley were dumbfounded. We celebrated our victory ecstatically. Well, all of us except Ross did: he disappeared with the speed of one of his own shots on goal, not stopping for a shower or a chat with anyone.

But he promised he'd be back for our next match – and he was. It was in that game, against fellow relegation candidates Bottle Lane, that we saw the first flash of the temper that could erupt like a volcano: and be just as destructive. Once again, we took an early lead with Ross volleying home from a clever pass from Scott, whose own play was beginning to flower as a result of his developing partnership with our new striker. The Laners are a tough lot and when Ross cannoned into one of their defenders as a corner kick was being taken the player retaliated by jabbing an elbow into Ross's stomach.

Instantaneously Ross lashed out with his fist and flattened the lad. By sheer good fortune the ref didn't see it and the linesman's view was partly obscured; Ross just got a ticking off instead of the booking that would have been automatic under other circumstances. However, the yellow card came out later when the two players tangled again and this time Ross was in full view of the ref when he kicked out at his opponent. The truth is he was lucky not to be sent off, although he didn't think so.

Before dashing off again after the final whistle he told everyone what he thought of the Bottle Lane player; the air turned blue. 'Next time he tries anything on me I'll put him in hospital,' Ross said. We all believed it was a firm promise. But we didn't think much more about it because Partley United had won again and we wanted to enjoy our new-found success.

Ross never joined in our social life; he claimed he wasn't even free for training, either, and his timing for our matches was so precise he never arrived early and he never lingered afterwards. 'You'd think he was on the run from prison or something like that,' Scott observed one night. Jason agreed.

'Yeah, he's the complete mystery man all right. But I don't care about that as long as he keeps knocking in the goals for us. That's the only thing that matters to me.'

Well, Ross's scoring touch didn't desert him in the following four matches and his goals lifted us clear of relegation worries. Our confidence soared. For the first time in months we could enjoy our football; we even reached the point where we expected to win every game. 'Next season,' we kept telling each other, 'we'll be going for promotion.'

Then we played Skelmorrie.

Within a minute of the kick-off Ross had the ball in the net, only for the 'goal' to be disallowed for what the ref indicated was a pushing offence. Ross practically went berserk, screaming at the referee that the goal was legitimate. Jason tried to intervene to calm things down but Ross wouldn't desist and so inevitably was booked for dissent.

'What's that lad's name?' asked the Skelmorrie winger standing beside me. I told him. 'Looks just like Jonny Anton to me,' was the response. 'Used to play for Kiltorver on the other side of the city. But he had long black hair then. He was really wild. Got banned for knocking a ref out. I played in that League last season. Kiltorver were useless after Anton went. But he'd've killed somebody if he'd stayed like that.'

I wanted to ask more but there was no time because the game restarted and the ball came my way. Skelmorrie were not a good side and I was confident we could beat them so long as Ross didn't do anything stupid; I could tell he was still simmering with resentment but that seemed to have evaporated after he'd scored two very good goals in a three-minute spell midway through the first half. The rest of us were jubilant. Ross Johnson was proving to be a goal-scoring machine – and he was on our side! Naturally, Skelmorrie were determined to prevent him getting a hat trick and so he came in for some fairly tough treatment whenever he got the ball – and the ball was finding its way to him like a pin drawn to a magnet.

Ross, to give him due credit, didn't complain about the hacking and the elbowing; in any case, he must have known that another flare up could easily result in his being sent off. A hat trick was what he wanted because, in spite of his consistent scoring, it was something he hadn't yet achieved for us. A minute before half-time he was positive he'd got that desirable third goal.

As it happened, I was the one who supplied him with the pass after I'd collected a loose ball in the centre circle and made uninterrupted progress to the edge of the box. Spotting Ross charging across from the right I sent over a cross which couldn't have been bettered: and Ross met it perfectly to head the ball over the keeper and into the net. We rushed towards each other to celebrate. Then, flabbergasted, I saw that the ref was signalling that it wasn't a goal. 'Offside, offside,' he declared. I didn't believe it and I don't think anyone else did, either. But he'd shown he wasn't a ref you could argue with.

Ross, however, was so incensed he'd probably forgotten that. He stormed towards the official and I wasn't the only one who thought he was about to murder him. Jason rushed to intervene. By now, Ross seemed to have lost all control. He was yelling that he was being robbed and cheated and ripped off and just about every other complaint you could imagine. Other players were trying to restrain him but suddenly he seemed to turn all his fury on Jason who was dragging on one of his arms. The punch he threw had a lot of power in it and Jason took it right on the chin. The thud as our skipper hit the ground must have been heard even by spectators on the far touchline.

For a moment, no one seemed to move. Then, perhaps because he was the nearest, Scott dived to Jason's aid.

We didn't have any medical help on standby, of course, and no one offered any assistance. So it was actually the ref himself who attended our skipper and managed to revive him. We were all thankful he knew what to do – and that Jason was shortly able to get to his feet again. He looked glassy-eyed and was unsteady but at least he wasn't seriously injured. (Weeks later, though, he was still suffering occasional twinges in his jaw.)

Then the ref turned his attention to Ross. Or, rather, that was his intention. But Ross was nowhere to be seen. He'd vanished. Fergus was the only one who'd seen what had happened. 'He just took off like a rocket as soon as Jason went down,' our goalie revealed. 'Went straight to the changing-room. Expect he guessed he'd be sent off, anyway.'

'He certainly will be when I get hold of him,' the ref agreed. 'Violent conduct like that's just got to be punished with all the rigour of the law. Sending-off's hardly sufficient. In my book he deserves a lengthy ban. If he can K.O. his own captain goodness knows what he might do to an opponent if he isn't stopped.'

Refs aren't usually so explicit in my experience but it showed how deeply he felt about the incident. Then the game was further held up while Fergus was sent to the changing-room to fetch Ross back so that he could be sent off officially. Not surprisingly, he wasn't there. Fergus reported that Ross's clothes had gone; and there was no sign of Ross himself.

'Well, he won't get away with this,' the ref promised. 'He won't be allowed to play for your team again until he's served his punishment. Like a runaway convict, he'll be on our wanted list until we catch up with him.'

I expected the Skelmorrie player, who'd told me about Ross's real identity, to inform the ref that Ross was really Jonny Anton, but he didn't say a word – perhaps because it wasn't one of their players who'd been attacked. I supposed the League would eventually trace Ross and he'd pay the penalty for his violence. But, until he lashed out at Jason, he'd certainly done us a good turn. His goals kept us out of trouble and they even enabled us to beat Skelmorrie, in spite of the fact that we played the rest of that game with only ten players (and one of them a fairly feeble substitute for poor old Jason).

None of us ever saw Ross again. But we did hear from him because he had the decency to return his Partley United number 9 shirt and shorts by post to my address. He even included a note: 'Sorry I had to run out on you. Hope Jason is OK and that United keep winning.' Naturally, there was no signature.

'He'd never have got away with it in a small town, you know,' Scott pointed out once when we discussed Ross, as we did regularly for weeks afterwards. 'He only dared do it because this is such a big city, where anybody can hide things about themselves.'

'Well, next time we advertise for a player we'll do a proper investigation into his background and then – ' Jason started to say.

'Next time?' Scott and I said in united disbelief.

Jason, rubbing his jaw thoughtfully, managed a wry grin. 'Well, it *did* work with Ross, didn't it?'

Alison Prince

Born in London 1931, of Scottish mother and Yorkshire father (whose job in the Yorkshire Bank had sent him unwillingly South). Educated at old-fashioned girls-only Grammar School, scholarship to London University, Slade School of Fine Art. Totally unable to get a job in Fine Art, worked in cafés, the Zoo, factories, and, in desperation, as an Art teacher – as a school-hater, I had vowed never to set foot in one again. Surprisingly, I loved teaching and found a great sympathy for even the most horrendous of children.

Marriage and birth of three children in quick succession stopped the teaching career. Broke, I began some freelance illustrating work and by sheer luck wrote a first story which became a television film, which led to a lot of TV work and to the writing of my first book, since when, others have followed in a fairly steady stream.

Falling on hard times in the 1970s, I bought a derelict farm in Suffolk, moved in with seven cats and the three children, now in their teens, and ran it for eight years, rearing calves, pigs, chickens and anything else which presented itself.

The children now being grown-up, I live very happily on the Isle of Arran with two dogs and a cat, and play the tuba in the brass band.

Matches

'Come straight home, won't you?' said Kellie's mother as she always did.

''Course I will,' Kellie said.

'Fiona will be there, won't she? You'll get a lift back with her mother?'

'I expect so,' said Kellie. Really, at almost twelve, it was time she was treated as having a little sense, she thought. Even if she *didn't* get a lift home, the Youth Club was only ten minutes' walk away. Kellie could not understand why her parents thought the streets were so dangerous after dark. She walked up and down them every day on her way to school, and saw nothing alarming – just people going to work or lugging Tesco bags full of shopping, and West Indian boys walking loose-kneed and finger-clicking to the music in their walkmans. None of them seemed dangerous. 'Come on,' she said impatiently. 'I'll be late.'

'So will I,' said Kellie's father. 'And *I'm* not going to a party, worse luck.' He looked very big in his police uniform, specially when he put his hat on.

'See you in the morning, love,' Kellie's mother said, kissing her husband. 'I hope you have a quiet night.'

It must be odd, working at night, Kellie thought, when everyone else is sleeping. She followed her father out of the flat to the lift. Rain began to blot against the balcony windows.

Several torches glowed under a pile of crumpled red tissue paper on the Church Hall floor. It did not look much like a bonfire. Mrs Peach handed out sparklers, long and grey at the end of their thin wires, and smiled at everyone. 'Cheer up!' she said. 'We can have a fire outside next week, if it's fine.'

'But it's Guy Fawkes night *tonight*,' Kellie pointed out. She had been looking forward to the Junior Youth Club's bonfire party for weeks. Bonfire party. The very words were exciting. Leaping flames, people's faces unfamiliar in the flickering firelight, the whizz and crackle of fireworks, the wonderful smells of sausages and gunpowder.

'The baked potatoes are in the microwave,' said Mrs Peach. 'They'll be ready in a minute.'

Outside, the rain continued to pour down. The Church Hall smelt of wet boys and stale tea, and loud pop music mixed with the unrhythmic clatter of ping-pong balls. Kellie felt cheated. She ate half a rather hard baked potato and sat down in the circle of people round the red paper fire-substitute while Mr Withers played his guitar and tried to get people to sing. The whole thing was a big disappointment.

To make it worse, when the Juniors packed up at half-past seven, the rain had stopped. The Seniors came in chattering triumphantly. 'Johnny Bennett's dad's brought a whole trailer-load of scrap timber,' Kellie heard one girl say to another. It was obvious that the Seniors were going to have a really terrific bonfire.

Kellie put on her anorak and felt the light rattle of the box of matches in its pocket. She had thought it was so sensible to bring matches. 'Oh, Kellie, what a practical girl you are!' Mrs Peach should have said as she struggled to get the fire lit in the drizzle. 'Thank you so much.' And the flames should have come snaking upward, triumphing over the rain.

Fiona had not turned up, probably because of the wet night. There would be no lift home. Kellie wondered whether to ask Mrs Peach if she could ring up home and ask her mother to come and meet her, then dismissed the thought. At nearly twelve, did she really need to be escorted home?

If I am accosted by some sinister stranger, Kellie thought as she set out, I shall strike a whole handful of matches like the little match girl in the story, and their unearthly radiance will make him hide his face and run away. She walked slowly, allowing the others to go ahead, dispersing on their various routes home. She knew she was being perverse – but the evening had been badly lacking in excitement, and the small adventure of walking home alone would help to make up for it. Just for a little while, she would be a night person, like her father.

She walked down the road where the orange street lights shone back from the puddles. There were distant crackles and bangs from other people's fireworks, and a rocket traced a fiery arc through the sky and was gone. Kellie turned the corner into the narrower street which her father called 'unsalubrious'. She wasn't sure what the word meant, but assumed that it had something to do with the boarded-up shops and the rubble-strewn spaces between buildings where down-and-outs gathered sometimes, to huddle like Bedouins of the desert among the stones and the fire-weed and the old packing cases, passing a bottle from hand to hand.

Someone was there now.

In the brown-shadowed darkness, Kellie could just make out the shape of a figure by the wall, stooping over something in the shelter of a shallow recess. It seemed a small figure, hardly taller than Kellie herself. It would probably be a bag-lady, Kellie thought – one of those old women who pushed a broken-down pram along the streets, full of the rubbish which was her household.

A firework burst into a fountain of silver stars in the sky, and Kellie saw that she was mistaken. The figure was a boy of about her own age, wearing short grey trousers which reached almost to his knees. The discovery gave her a sense of relief. She was not exactly afraid of the bag-ladies, but this boy seemed wonderfully harmless. In the quivering glow of a pink Roman Candle, she saw how thin his bare legs were, ending in falling-down socks and big boots.

The boy looked up and saw her. 'Have you got a match?' he called. 'I want to get this fire lit.'

Kellie felt a surge of pride and pleasure. So her matches *were* needed, after all! 'Yes, I have,' she called back.

The boy trod his way across the rubble towards her. In addition to the grey shorts, he wore a skinny jersey whose sleeves did not come to his wrists. He must be cold, Kellie thought. 'I've got it all built,' he said, 'over there where it's sheltered from the rain. But I couldn't light it. I'd be really glad if you'd help.'

He turned away, back towards the alcove in the wall, as if assuming that she would follow him. Kellie hesitated for a moment. Her parents had warned her again and again about speaking to strangers, and she had overheard snatches of conversation between them about dreadful things her father had seen in his duty as a policeman – though he always stopped when he noticed Kellie was listening, and smiled at her instead, and asked if she'd had a good day at school. But this boy was not a criminal. He was not even a grown-up, and he sounded so polite as to be almost old-fashioned.

Kellie picked her way across the stones and cinders to where the boy stood and waited for her beside the carefully-built bonfire. There, she crouched and struck a match. She cupped it in her hands to protect the wavering yellow flame, and applied it to the crumpled paper which waited in the centre of the scrap-wood pyramid. An edge caught alight, curling as the flame licked along it, and Kellie moved the still-burning match to a new place, touching it to another corner of newspaper.

Smoke began to rise from the pile, and the smaller sticks crackled and burned, making a red cavern within the stacked wood. The boy held his hands to the blaze, crouching on his heels. 'I like fire,' he said, and his thin face was eager as he stared into the flames.

'So do I,' said Kellie. The evening had not been a total disaster, after all. This private Guy Fawkes bonfire was like a prize awarded when all had seemed lost.

'Sometimes,' the boy went on dreamily, 'you can imagine being in it. Part of it.'

Kellie was startled. 'As if you were burning?'

'No.' The boy shook his head. 'It's got these caves, all red and glowing. You could walk about in them. Go up to heaven in the smoke. I'd like to be in there. Better than this.'

He sat back, hugging his knees, and the firelight flickered across his face as he stared unblinkingly at the glow. 'What's your name?' Kellie asked curiously.

'Edwin. Edwin Gathercole.'

Kellie laughed. 'That's nice. Gather coal for a fire. It suits you. I'm Kellie Brown.'

'How do you do,' said the boy, and leaned across to shake hands formally.

Again, it struck Kellie that there was something slightly old-fashioned about him. Maybe he had very severe parents, she thought, who fussed a lot about manners – but, in that case, what was he doing out here all by himself? 'Where do you live?' she asked.

'I was in the home,' the boy said, and dropped his chin to his knees, still hugging his legs as he continued to stare hungrily into the fire.

'But you're not now?' Kellie prompted after a pause.

Edwin gave a slight shrug. 'I am too old,' he said, as if it was obvious.

Kellie was puzzled. Surely children's homes kept people until they had left school and were old enough to look after themselves? 'But you must live some-where,' she objected.

Edwin turned his head and looked at her steadily, and there was something likeable about his snub nose and wide mouth, and the straight eyes. 'There is no "must" about it,' he said. 'I have lived in all sorts of places, where people have put me. But I shall be free now. Free to mix with the air and be part of everything.' He turned back to smile at the fire, and again stretched his bony hands to it.

As the flames mounted, the flickering firelight leapt across the ruined walls and the old packing cases and rubble, and fireworks burst intermittently in the sky, sometimes with the whoosh of a rocket or the crackle of sparkling explosions, sometimes with the silent blossoming of starry flowers.

Suddenly Kellie gave a gasp. For the first time, she saw that she and the boy were not alone. On the far side of the fire, looking like a dark heap of rags, an old man lay huddled on his side, with his knees drawn up and a slack-fingered hand lying protectively across an empty bottle. The eyes in his grey face glittered in the firelight, and he was perfectly still.

Kellie scrambled to her feet in alarm – and in the same instant, she saw that the boy was not there.

'Edwin!' she tried to scream, but no sound came from her except a breathless yelp, like an animal in pain. Where was he? In that brief moment, there had been no time for him to get up and go away. Had she imagined the whole thing? Was she dreaming? A billow of smoke enveloped her and made her eyes smart, and she buried her face in her anorak sleeve. This was real. She could feel the heat of the fire on her hands and her legs, and hear its crackling. As the smoke cleared and she looked up again, the movement of her arm made the box of matches shift in her pocket.

The old man's face had not changed, but the open eyes glowed with a weird greenness. Kellie was suddenly more afraid than she had ever been in her life. The leaping firelight seemed like a crazy dance of mocking shadows, and a burst of fire-crackers from a nearby garden seemed to emphasise the stillness of the huddled thing which had been a man. She should not be in this place. She should have gone straight home. Guilt mixed with her terror, and Kellie turned and ran, stumbling over loose stones and half-bricks, with the box of matches jumping in her pocket.

Someone was coming along the pavement towards her.

'*Kellie! There* you are! Where on earth have you

been?' Kellie found herself enfolded in her mother's arms. 'What happened? Didn't Fiona's mother come? Oh, darling, what is it?'

Kellie sobbed and shivered, and her mother kept up a stream of frantic questions. What had she been doing? Had anyone hurt her? What had happened?

'It was the boy,' Kellie blurted. 'He wanted a match. And we couldn't have a proper bonfire at the Youth Club because of the rain.'

'What boy?' Her mother sounded even more worried. 'A big boy, d'you mean? A grown-up?'

'No, he was about twelve. Edwin Gathercole. But he went. And there was this old man – ' Kellie pointed briefly. 'Over there, by the fire.'

'Did he do anything to you?'

Kellie shook her head and gave a hiccupping laugh which was almost a sob. The man could not do anything at all. 'He's lying there. I think he's – ' Somehow, she could not say the word.

Kellie's mother advanced a few paces across the rough ground and stared at the old man. The fire was beginning to die down for lack of fresh fuel. 'Oh, my goodness,' she said. 'Come along, Kellie, we'd better get home. I'll ring Daddy at the station.'

Walking beside her mother through the orange-lit streets and the smell of fireworks, Kellie began to feel calmer. 'There *was* a boy,' she said, only half aware that she spoke aloud.

'Never mind about it now,' said her mother. 'Just as long as you're not hurt.'

'I'm all right,' said Kellie.

'You should have rung me from the Youth Club,' said her mother. 'I'll have something to say to Mrs Peach, letting you go off on your own like that.'

'It wasn't her fault,' said Kellie.

Her mother went on scolding and worrying, but Kellie hardly heard. She had a lot to think about.

At home, Kellie sat by the kitchen table with a mug of drinking chocolate. Her mother came back from telephoning in the next room and said, 'Off to bed with you, if you've finished that. School in the morning. I'll come and tuck you in.'

Kellie was half asleep when she heard the police car's siren and saw a blue light flash repeatedly across the ceiling. She sat up in bed and looked out of the window. From her room in the high flat, she could see down between the buildings to the bit of waste land where a small red fire still glowed. The blue light was on top of an ambulance, and a police car had drawn up behind it. The sound of its radio came with strange loudness through the dark, though the words were incomprehensible. People with powerful torches were stooping over something. One of them, Kellie saw, was her father. Then they went back to the ambulance and brought out a stretcher. Kellie caught a glimpse of red blanket as they carried a burden back to the ambulance and slid it smoothly in. The old man, she thought. She watched until the ambulance drove away, followed by the police car. The small red fire was no more than a speck in the darkness. From behind the flats, a last rocket soared into the sky, burst with a faint pop and disintegrated into a silent shower of sparks. Kellie gave a shiver and lay down again, snuggling into the bedclothes. Free now, she thought, remembering the boy's words without understanding them. Free to mix with the air and be part of everything. And then she was asleep.

* * *

They were having breakfast the next morning when
Kellie's father came in, tired and unshaven after his
night's work. 'Well, young lady,' he said to Kellie as he
sat down at the table and stirred the cup of tea his wife
put in front of him. 'A fine dance you led us last night.
What on earth did you think you were doing? That's
exactly the kind of unsalubrious place you should keep
away from. And people like that, too. Drop-outs,
junkies, alcoholics – they are the dregs, Kellie. *Horrible*
people. You really must keep away from them.'

Kellie felt her eyes fill with tears. Edwin had not been
horrible. He looked a bit comic, with his long shorts
and his falling-down socks and big boots, but there had
been something very nice about the grave way he spoke
to her, and the directness of the eyes in that thin face.

'Don't cry, darling,' said her mother kindly. 'We're
not cross with you. But I hope you've learned your
lesson. You won't ever do that again, will you?'

Kellie shook her head. It couldn't happen a second
time. But there was something she had to know. 'Was
the old man dead?' she asked. It seemed easier to say the
word in the brisk sunlight of the morning, with cornflakes and marmalade on the table.

Her parents glanced at each other. Then Kellie's father
said, 'Yes, he was, love, but you mustn't worry about it
too much. When people get to that kind of state, they're
better off out of it.'

Better than this, Kellie thought, remembering Edwin's
words. With only the faintest of hopes, she asked, 'Did
you see a boy? About the same age as me, in shorts?'

Her father shook his head. 'You don't get children
round these places, they'd be taken into care. If there
was a boy, he'd no business to be there, any more than
you had. No, there was just the old chap. Edwin

Gathercole, his name was – we found his pension book in his pocket. I looked up his record. Brought up in a home, terrible history of borstal and prison – he was a compulsive fire-raiser. Kept burning places down.'

The daylight seemed to do a somersault, and Kellie felt the blood drain from her face, leaving her shaky and weak. She put her piece of bread and marmalade carefully down on the plate, unable to take another mouthful.

'You mentioned someone called Edwin Gathercole last night, didn't you, Kellie?' said her mother with curiosity. 'Did the old man tell you his name?'

Kellie did not answer. Confusion raged in her mind. 'I am too old,' Edwin had said. In the dying minutes of an old man's life, had his spirit reverted to the boy he had been? Such a nice boy, with straight eyes and old-fashioned courtesy – and a passion for fire. What had happened in the years between, to turn the boy into a derelict old man?

'Useful if he, did speak to you,' Kellie's father was saying with professional interest. 'Fixes the time of death. *Did* he say anything, Kellie?'

'I – I just thought I heard the name,' said Kellie. Did it matter now? Edwin had no existence, except in her own memory.

Her father sighed, and her mother said briskly, 'You'd better get off to school, love. Got your dinner money?'

'Yes, thank you,' said Kellie.

'Want to finish your bread and marmalade?'

'No, thanks.'

'Are you feeling all right?'

'Yes.'

But Kellie felt strange. Outside the window of the flat, the clear sky contained, she knew, invisible traces of last night's smoke, from Edwin's bonfire and from all the other bonfires lit by people like the Senior Youth Club. Today, the smoke had disappeared, absorbed invisibly into the air, and Edwin Gathercole had disappeared as well, leaving only the body of some down-and-out old man, to be taken away in an ambulance.

Kellie went down in the lift and walked along the street, such a different place now in the morning light, with bits of paper and crisp bags blowing merrily about. In a few minutes, she came to the derelict site of last night, and paused to look at it. A small grey patch of ash surrounded by a few charred sticks was all that remained of Edwin's fire.

Over by the wall, a bag-lady rocked and crooned as she picked through the contents of a plastic carrier she held on her lap, grey hair falling in matted snarls over her shoulders. 'People like that are the dregs,' Kellie's father had said. But the boy who had been Edwin Gathercole was clear in Kellie's mind, standing at her side in the darkness. This grey-haired woman, too, had once been a child – a little girl who had not known where her life's path would lead her.

Kellie's eyes stung with tears at the pity of it all. She groped in her pocket for a handkerchief, and found the box of matches, firm and light in her fingers. Carefully, she bent down and laid it on a brick among the rubble. It was not much, but it was the best she could do. She saw the old woman look up with the quick interest of a ruffle-feathered blackbird which has spotted a worm, and backed away, for, despite the pity, she was a little afraid.

Penny Boyle and Debbie Craig waved and shouted to her from the other side of the street, and Kellie waited for a gap in the traffic then crossed over to join them.

She did not look back to see the old woman picking up the matches. She and Penny and Debbie ran all the way to school in the bright morning, which held no threat for the future, and no promise.

Bernard MacLaverty

I began writing shortly after leaving school. I don't know why. I had tried my hand at some poems but the first story I attempted was about my grandmother and her big black handbag and how she took it up to bed with her as if she didn't trust the rest of the family. It was only a page long but I enjoyed doing it. It probably was very bad (I've since lost it) and so were the stories I wrote over the next ten years. They were all copies of writers I admired. Then one day I wrote my own story in my own voice and that was a second beginning.

Since then I have written two novels and three collections of short stories. Some of these I have turned into radio plays, some into television plays and the two novels into films.

Writing for younger readers began with my own children. They plagued me to tell them stories and I wrote some of them down and drew very clumsy pictures to illustrate them. But we have a book now in our house that nobody else in the world has a copy of. Occasionally, now that my children have grown-up, they take the book out and laugh at it.

The Mystery of the Beehive

The boy stood on the deck waving to his mother as the boat pulled out. He waved until she became a small figure with an upturned, white face. The dockside buildings began to get smaller and smaller and gave Brendan a strange feeling of loneliness. It was the first time he had ever been away from home by himself. He thrust his hands deep into his anorak pockets and spat over the side. When it hit the wind the spit turned at a sharp right-angle.

At school they had been reading about the potato famine and he imagined himself as one of the exiles, one of the people who had had to leave or else starve to death. The teacher had said that an exile was somebody who had to leave his native country when he didn't want to. Brendan felt like that now.

He was going on holiday to Scotland to his uncle's farm – a man he had only met once before in his life. There would be nobody to play with because his uncle and aunt had no children. But his mother had insisted that he should get away from the streets of Belfast for at least part of the summer.

The wind blew his hair and he felt cold enough to shiver. He went into the lounge, found a seat and ate the sandwiches his mother had made for him. He wondered what the farm would be like. With a small start of panic he wondered what would happen if his uncle didn't recognise him when he got to the other side.

But he needn't have worried. His Uncle Michael was there at the quayside, waving and smiling. When they met they shook hands awkwardly. His uncle's hand was huge and as rough as sandpaper.

There was a smell of pigs in the car as they drove northwards through the town and out into the country where yellow broom, the colour of butter, grew all along the side of the road. Brendan sat forward so that he could see his uncle's face better. He hadn't shaved and his chin was all bristly with copper-coloured hairs. His cap was pulled down almost to his nose so that to see to drive he had to tilt his head back. Uncle Michael talked in a loud voice asking him how his parents were and how they were standing up to the troubles in Belfast. He asked Brendan if his da had grown any hair on his baldy head.

Brendan laughed, 'Have you got any hair, Uncle Michael?'

'I have, but it's all round the edges,' he said and lifted his cap to show his bald dome sticking up through the red hair.

As they drove along, the smell of pigs became so awful that Brendan asked if he could open a window. No sooner had he opened it than the car was filled with a buzzing noise. Brendan cowered back as the insect dashed itself from one window to another.

'It's only a bee,' said his uncle, looking round at him. But when he saw how frightened the boy was he stopped the car and shooed it out with his hand.

'I'm not afraid of bees,' said Brendan, but his voice was shaking and he looked a bit pale.

'You don't have to be tough with me,' said his uncle.

'It takes a brave man to be afraid. You'll have to get used to them because there are bees on the farm.'

When they arrived, Brendan was a bit disappointed. He didn't know what he had expected but it wasn't this. A scatter of red-leaded outbuildings, a paved yard, the house itself. It was old – a bungalow type with attic rooms sticking out of the roof. His Aunt Betty met him at the door with a big smile, wiping her hands on her apron.

'Come in,' she said. 'You must be starving.'

As they sat down to the neatly-laid table Uncle Michael laughed and said, 'Somebody important must be coming. We've got the tablecloth on.'

Without saying a word Aunt Betty took his cap off and set it on the radio then hit him a tiny slap on his bald head. 'Get on with your tea,' she said.

Brendan was just trying to answer Aunt Betty's questions and eat at the same time when he heard a heavy thumping step in the hallway. The door opened and Brendan stared, his eyes widening. A masked figure stood on the threshold. The figure was dressed in white – wide-brimmed white hat, white smock, white gloves and a white nylon mask covering his face.

When Uncle Michael saw Brendan's face he laughed and said, 'There's no need to worry – you're not in Belfast now. This is Mr Zveginzov. He's our bee-keeper.'

Brendan laughed, feeling a bit ashamed. Mr Zveginzov took off his gloves, then his hat with the covering muslin. He was very old and slightly stooped. He had a blunt face and his hair was white and stubble-cut. His mouth was pulled down sourly at the corners. The eyelid of his left eye drooped, like a half-drawn window blind. He nodded brusquely to the new guest, then stomped heavily up the stairs to his room. In his hand Brendan noticed a small canvas bag.

'You mustn't worry about Zveginzov,' said Aunt Betty. 'He's a little bit odd, but he's very nice really. He has his routines, his little ways.'

'And you can't blame him,' said Uncle Michael, 'he's been through a lot.'

'Yes,' Aunt Betty nodded. 'He just called at the door one night. He wanted to work for something to eat. We took him in and he's been a sort of boarder ever since.'

Brendan asked about his funny name and Aunt Betty told him that Mr Zveginzov was a Jew who had lived in Russia a long time ago. He had left his country because of the pogroms.

'The what?' asked Brendan.

'Pogroms,' said his aunt. 'That's just another name for a sort of riot. Some Russian people hated the Jews and they stoned them and beat them. They drove them out of their homes and even killed them because they were Jewish.'

'I know,' said Brendan.

'So Zveginzov ran away from Russia and wandered the world until the night he ended up here. Be kind and polite to him and you should get on well together.'

After tea Brendan went out to play and explore the farm. Beyond the paved yard were the open fields and the hills covered in patches of gorse, yellow on dark green. Higher on the hillside it gave way to purple heather. A small trout stream, brown and crystal and flecked with foam, splashed its crooked way down from the mountain.

On his way back to the house he discovered a long vegetable garden. At the bottom was a clear area with six beehives sitting on the grass. Brendan sat and watched from a safe distance the bees coming and going. The air was filled with their constant buzzing drone. He thought of the man's funny name and said it over and over again. He loved repeating words – even the simplest ones – until they lost their meaning.

'Zveginzov, Zveginzov, Zveginzov.' He thought it sounded like the bees. 'Zveginzov.' He pulled and chewed a stalk of grass. Already he was a bit bored.

He went back to the house just as his Aunt Betty was finishing the dishes. 'Which room am I sleeping in?' he asked.

Aunt Betty dried her hands on the roller towel on the back of the door and led him through the hallway. 'Your room is downstairs at the back of the house,' she said.

Brendan looked out through the small panes of the window. Outside was a beautiful tree. He couldn't remember seeing one like it ever. It was small and looked old and gnarled but its yellow beaded blossoms hung down like gold, like necklaces.

'What sort of tree is that?' he asked.

'Oh yes, I'm glad you reminded me. Good boy, Brendan. You must never touch that tree because it's poisonous. It's a laburnum tree and if you ate one of those seeds – out of the little black pods – you would be dead before you could eat another one. With no children about the place you forget how dangerous it is. Promise me now you won't touch it.'

Brendan nodded and said over and over to himself, 'Laburnum, laburnum, laburnum' until it had no meaning.

'Another thing,' said Aunt Betty, pointing her finger at the ceiling, 'that's Mr Zveginzov's room straight above you, so you must be as quiet as a mouse when he's in. All right?'

Brendan nodded and asked if he could go upstairs to explore but to his surprise his aunt answered sharply. 'No. You mustn't go upstairs and disturb Mr Zveginzov. This is his private time. He has asked us specially and we have agreed to it. That's another promise you'll have to keep.' Then she smiled at herself for having spoken so sharply. 'He's old,' she said, 'and not used to children.'

That night, as he lay in the strange bed with its faintly damp smell, Brendan couldn't sleep for hours. Outside the window the blossoms of the poisonous laburnum swung in the night breeze silently. He heard Mr Zveginzov come in and go up the creaking stairway. Above his head the heavy footsteps crossed and recrossed the floor for what seemed like most of the night. Brendan looked at the ceiling and saw the light-bulb tremble slightly at each step and wondered what was wrong with the old man.

The next day Brendan went to play on the haystacks in the field beside the vegetable garden. The sun came out and it was warm. The hay looked yellow and soft but when he tried to climb a haystack he found it hard and prickly. There was a small ladder against one stack and Brendan climbed this to slide down the other side. When he was on the top he could see over the hedge into the vegetable garden. He saw Mr Zveginzov come out of the house dressed in his beekeeper's clothes. Brendan slid down the haystack and crawled into the bottom of the hedge. He could see quite clearly Zveginzov walking empty-handed to the hives and when he opened one a black swarm of bees raced out and hovered around his head. They crawled on his hat and the nylon

Bernard MacLaverty

mask covering his face but he didn't seem to mind. Brendan shuddered at the thought of it – their furry bodies, their buzzing wings.

When Zveginzov came to the third hive he opened it with particular care. Brendan watched closely. Zveginzov crouched down and took out a small canvas bag. It was the same bag Brendan had seen him bring into the house the afternoon before. The old man stood up slowly and put his gloved hand to his back as if he was in pain. Then he walked through the vegetable garden back to the house carrying the canvas bag.

Brendan followed him back to the house and got in just in time to hear Zveginzov's footsteps going up the stairs to his room. Aunt Betty was baking some scones and he knew that he would be caught if he tried to sneak up after him. Besides he had made a promise that he wouldn't go up the stairs.

He went outside and sat in the garden looking up at Zveginzov's bedroom window. He hadn't pulled his curtains. The branches of the laburnum tree reached up and almost tapped the window pane. The hanging yellow flowers swayed in the light breeze. Brendan got up off the grass and went over to the tree. As he reached up his hand he thought of his aunt's warning. 'You mustn't even touch it.' He closed his hand round one of the flowers slowly and crushed it. He waited. He knew that touching a flower couldn't kill him.

It was an easy tree to climb, its branches old with plenty of grips for his hands and feet. As he climbed, the tree began to shake and all the hanging flowers trembled under his weight. He reached the branch level with Zveginzov's window. It was hard to see into the room because the sun had gone behind a cloud.

Gradually he made out Zveginzov's figure. He was

slumped over the table with his face buried in his arms. On the table was the canvas bag – open but Brendan couldn't see into it. Then the old man moved. He ran his fingers through his short stubbly white hair and nodded his head from side to side. Then he dipped into the bag and took something out of it. He looked at it closely but it was shielded from Brendan by his hand. Zveginzov looked down into the bag. The sun came out from behind the cloud, shining into the room, and Brendan saw a bright yellow reflected from the bag into the old man's face.

Zveginzov smiled, then suddenly he looked up and saw Brendan watching him from the tree. In a flash his look changed to one of anger and he jumped over to the window, his face white. Brendan leapt from the tree through a hiss of leaves and ran. He heard Zveginzov open the window and scream something after him but he didn't know what it was because it was in a different language.

All day Brendan sneaked about the house avoiding Mr Zveginzov and the next morning when he got up the old man had gone out. Aunt Betty set a plateful of her home-made scones on the breakfast table, then brought a section of honey to put on them. It was like a little wooden box, open at the top. Inside was a network of a white substance shaped like chicken wire.

'What's that?' asked Brendan.

'Beeswax,' said Aunt Betty. 'The bees make those little cells and then fill them with honey. You can eat that stuff. It's nice and crunchy.' Brendan dipped his knife into the honeycomb and spread some on his scone.

'Yes, the honey here is a good flavour because of the heather,' said Aunt Betty. 'And Mr Zveginzov looks after them well. It's like gold, isn't it? The colour I mean.'

'Where is Mr Zveginzov?' asked Brendan.

'I think he's gone to town. He goes to town every Friday,' she said, and left him to eat his breakfast. As he ate, Brendan thought about the canvas bag. What could be in it? Why did the old man hide it in the beehives? By the time he had finished his breakfast he had decided that there was only one way to find out.

He tiptoed into the hallway, lifted Zveginzov's bee-keeping clothes that were hanging there and slipped into the vegetable garden. He put on the straw hat and made it fit by tying it tight with the mask. Then the smock, which hung down over his wrists. The gloves had elastic cuffs to stop the bees crawling up the sleeves but they were too loose on Brendan. Now he was scared and shaking a little. He had heard of people who died from bee-stings. As he came near the hives the sound of the bees grew louder and louder. One or two flew into the mask protecting his face and he brushed them away with his glove.

The sun was shining and he became very hot and uncomfortable under all the clothes. He felt sweat on his upper lip. He reached the third hive and rested his hand on it. Immediately thousands of bees, with what sounded like a roar, came streaming out of the hive and encircled his head. He clenched his teeth. So many bees had come out that he thought the hive must be empty. But when he opened it thousands more poured out, their furry black and yellow bodies bumping into his veil, crawling over his chest and shoulders.

He looked into the hive past the swirling bees but could see no canvas bag. It was in the next hive that he found it. Immediately he turned and ran with it to the house end of the garden. When he was sure that no bees had followed him he took off the hat and mask. The gloves made his hands too clumsy to open the bag so he had to pull them off. It was closed with a draw-string at the neck. His excited fingers fumbled with the cord.

Brendan was so interested in the canvas bag that he didn't notice a movement behind him. Then a twig snapped under the weight of someone's foot. Brendan looked up. Zveginzov stood over him. His lips were drawn back in anger and his eyelid half drooped – like the blind in a house where someone has just died. He snatched the bag from Brendan.

'You nosey brat!' he shouted. Brendan thought he was going to strike him with his upraised hand but instead he rubbed the short white hair of his head. Suddenly the old man's face crumpled up and he began to cry. Brendan stood watching him, not knowing what to do. The tears ran down Zveginzov's face. He squatted down on the ground and when he spoke the anger had gone out of his voice.

'It you want to know so much what's in the bag, I will show you.' He opened it and let the boy look in. A hoard of gold coins gleamed at the bottom. Zveginzov took one out. It had strange writing on it around an eagle with spread wings. He turned it over and on the other side was a man's head.

'That is the Tsar's head,' he said. 'What I hold is a gold rouble. The only thing that I take with me out of Russia.' The tears were still wet on his face. Brendan repeated to himself the word 'Rouble, rouble, rouble' until it had no meaning.

'And here is something else,' said Zveginzov, taking a tiny bag out of the larger one. 'Do you know what is in that?'

Brendan opened it. There was some dirt at the bottom of it but nothing else.

'It is the soil of Russia.' Brendan looked at him, not understanding. 'Let me tell you then. You left your own country to come here, is that not so? Do you know how you would have been feeling if you had to leave it for ever?' Brendan nodded. 'How would you feel if you had nothing to make you remember? I took these roubles, I took this – how do you say – handful of soil to remind me of my dear, dear Russia.' The tears came to his eyes again.

'But if you loved it so much why did you leave it?'

'You ask me why I leave,' said Zveginzov. 'When somebody they burn your house from over your head, when somebody they kill your mother, when everybody they stone and spit at you – you do not stay in that place. It is time to go. I was the age of you, maybe, when my Papa took me and my brother and we ran. He gave me this bag to carry because he knew soldiers would stop him with his black beard and his face of a Jew. And they did. The soldiers they killed my brother and Papa. Me they did not kill because I hid in a cellar. You ask me why I leave? You see this eye. I tell you how my eye happened. My brother and my Papa lie dead on the street. There is dust in his beard and my brother's eyes they are open. There is a little sign around my Papa's neck telling the world he is a Jew. I go to them to say goodbye and I kneel in the dust of the street. And what happens? A boy of my own age – of your age – sees me and lifts a stone, as sharp as a knife, and he throws it in my eye. Then he spits for hate of me. I run and I do not know where I am running because my eye is as full of blood as his heart is full of hate. And you ask me why I leave?'

Brendan looked at his drooping eyelid and the blank staring eye behind it. He asked, 'But why did you keep your gold in the beehive?'

'Memories you cannot keep in a bank. I want to see my roubles. Each day I want to touch my soil. Where is gold safer than in a beehive?' The old man shrugged his shoulders and put his hands on his head. Brendan cleared his throat and said that he was sorry.

Zveginzov smiled. 'To be young is to be nosey,' he said. 'But you must keep my secret.' Zveginzov dipped two fingers into the bag and produced a gold coin which he gave to Brendan. He made him promise never to spend it, but to keep it all his life to remember an old man who had lost his country.

TAKE YOUR KNEE OFF MY HEART

Miriam Hodgson (editor)

'Love demands songs, really.'

David Johnstone

'We usually make complete idiots of ourselves when we fall in love.'

Mary Hooper

'Love has a way of reaching into every corner of our daily lives.'

Marjorie Darke

Nine superb new love stories to make you laugh and cry, including stories by Marjorie Darke, Mary Hooper, Monica Hughes, Pete Johnson, David Johnstone, Anthony Masters, Jenny Nimmo, Ann Pilling and Dyan Sheldon.

ONE STEP BEYOND

Pete Johnson

Sometimes you're walking right on the edge and don't even realise it.

Like Alex. He's waited five years to take revenge on Mr Stones.

And Natasha. She's always done what her parents tell her – until the day she turns sixteen.

Then there's Yorga. He has a brilliant idea to stop the hated Casuals taking over his town.

Just three of the people who don't realise they're right on the edge – until they take one step beyond.

A collection of eight dazzling stories of love, revenge, laughter and horror.

'Pete Johnson, an author who can pinpoint what is distinctive about his readers . . . without being either patronising or strait-jacketed by their demands.'

Sunday Times

'Pete Johnson's work is changing while his teenage voice is always authentic.'

Glasgow Herald

UNINVITED GHOSTS

Penelope Lively

What would you do if a ghost not only sat in your room every night knitting, but asked its friends and relations along as well? Or if a Martian got stranded in your back garden? Or if you wished you could have this all over again – and your wish came true?

All kinds of strange things can happen to perfectly ordinary people – and they *do*, in these ingenious and funny tales, with a surprise at every turn.

A collection of intriguing and witty stories by the author of the Carnegie-winning *The Ghost of Thomas Kempe*.

'All the authentic Lively qualities, of engagement, fun, observation . . . a book to cherish, to read again and again, and to lend to others at your peril – they'll never give it back.'

Junior Bookshelf

THE WHITE HORSE OF ZENNOR

Michael Morpurgo

Once a year, on a misty autumn night, there is a pounding of hoofbeats and a great white horse comes thundering over the moor in the moonlight. It is a reminder of the knocker's promise: the little old man whose life Arthur and Annie saved and who in return saved their father's farm from ruin.

Then there are the old tin miners, still busy in the abandoned mine, that Cherry meets when in her search for shells she's cut off by the incoming tide . . .

And 'Limping Billy', the crippled boy whom all the other children taunt, who learns to swim with the seals and finally goes to join them . . .

Five haunting tales by a master storyteller whose previous novels include *Why the Whales Came*, *Waiting for Anya* and *Mr Nobody's Eyes*.

A Selected List of Fiction from Mammoth

While every effort is made to keep prices low, it is sometimes necessary to increase prices at short notice. Mandarin Paperbacks reserves the right to show new retail prices on covers which may differ from those previously advertised in the text or elsewhere.

The prices shown below were correct at the time of going to press.

☐	7497 0978 2	**Trial of Anna Cotman**	Vivien Alcock	£2.50
☐	7497 0712 7	**Under the Enchanter**	Nina Beachcroft	£2.50
☐	7497 0106 4	**Rescuing Gloria**	Gillian Cross	£2.50
☐	7497 0035 1	**The Animals of Farthing Wood**	Colin Dann	£3.50
☐	7497 0613 9	**The Cuckoo Plant**	Adam Ford	£3.50
☐	7497 0443 8	**Fast From the Gate**	Michael Hardcastle	£1.99
☐	7497 0136 6	**I Am David**	Anne Holm	£2.99
☐	7497 0295 8	**First Term**	Mary Hooper	£2.99
☐	7497 0033 5	**Lives of Christopher Chant**	Diana Wynne Jones	£2.99
☐	7497 0601 5	**The Revenge of Samuel Stokes**	Penelope Lively	£2.99
☐	7497 0344 X	**The Haunting**	Margaret Mahy	£2.99
☐	7497 0537 X	**Why The Whales Came**	Michael Morpurgo	£2.99
☐	7497 0831 X	**The Snow Spider**	Jenny Nimmo	£2.99
☐	7497 0992 8	**My Friend Flicka**	Mary O'Hara	£2.99
☐	7497 0525 6	**The Message**	Judith O'Neill	£2.99
☐	7497 0410 1	**Space Demons**	Gillian Rubinstein	£2.50
☐	7497 0151 X	**The Flawed Glass**	Ian Strachan	£2.99

All these books are available at your bookshop or newsagent, or can be ordered direct from the publisher. Just tick the titles you want and fill in the form below.

Mandarin Paperbacks, Cash Sales Department, PO Box 11, Falmouth, Cornwall TR10 9EN.

Please send cheque or postal order, no currency, for purchase price quoted and allow the following for postage and packing:

UK including BFPO — £1.00 for the first book, 50p for the second and 30p for each additional book ordered to a maximum charge of £3.00.

Overseas including Eire — £2 for the first book, £1.00 for the second and 50p for each additional book thereafter.

NAME (Block letters) ....

ADDRESS ....

....

☐ I enclose my remittance for ....

☐ I wish to pay by Access/Visa Card Number ☐☐☐☐ ☐☐☐☐ ☐☐☐☐ ☐☐☐☐

Expiry Date ☐☐☐☐